'In Esther Kinsky, German literature has an author whose books are full of poetic intelligence.... A brilliant new novel.'
—*Neue Zürcher Zeitung*

'Esther Kinsky has created a literary oeuvre of impressive stylistic brilliance, thematic diversity and stubborn originality.... [T]he radical view of the loner resumes its place in literature: wandering, observing, feeling their way out of an initial state of strangeness, Kinsky's narrators regard human stories as a mere part of the natural history in which they are embedded. Although the Earth's movements and geology, flora and fauna are given uncommon attention, the popular term "nature writing" by no means adequately describes this work. As far as setting is concerned, the author deems no material unworthy... it is always clear that for her the only landscape worth describing is the one in which she is currently situated. Far from "eco-dreaming", without sorrow or critique, Kinsky's novels and poems position humanity in relation to the ruins it has produced and what still remains of nature.'
—2022 Kleist Prize jury

Rombo

ESTHER KINSKY

Translated from the German by Caroline Schmidt

nyrb **New York Review Books** New York

This is a New York Review Book

published by The New York Review of Books

435 Hudson Street, New York, NY 10014

www.nyrb.com

The translation of this work was supported by
a grant from the Goethe-Institut London.

Originally published by Fitzcarraldo Editions in Great Britain in 2022.

LIBRARY OF CONGRESS CATALOGING-IN-PUBLICATION DATA
Names: Kinsky, Esther, author. | Schmidt, Caroline, translator.
Title: Rombo / Esther Kinsky; translation by Caroline Schmidt.
Other titles: Rombo. English
Description: New York: New York Review Books, [2022]
Identifiers: LCCN 2022018703 (print) | LCCN 2022018704 (ebook) |
ISBN 9781681377247 (paperback) | ISBN 9781681377254 (ebook)
Subjects: LCGFT: Novels.
Classification: LCC PT2711.I67 R6613 2022 (print) |
LCC PT2711.I67 (ebook) | DDC 833/.92—dc23/eng/20220426
LC record available at https://lccn.loc.gov/2022018703
LC ebook record available at https://lccn.loc.gov/2022018704

ISBN 978-1-68137-724-7
Available as an electronic book; ISBN 978-1-68137-725-4

Printed in the United States of America on acid-free paper

10 9 8 7 6 5 4 3 2 1

'Finito questo, la buia campagna tremò sì forte, che dello spavento la mente di sudore ancor mi bagna. La terra lagrimosa diede vento, che balenò una luce vermiglia la qual mi vins ciascun sentiment.'
—DANTE ALIGHIERI, *La Commedia, Inferno*,
Canto III, v. 130–135.

'Unbeknownst to me at the time, I just wanted
to be seen.'
—C. FAUSTO CABRERA, *The Parameters of Our Cage*

I

'One of the few phenomena that almost always accompany an earthquake, and often announce its arrival shortly beforehand, consists of a curious subterranean sound, seemingly of the same nature almost everywhere it is given mention. This sound consists of the rolling tones of a row of suspended explosions, and is often compared to the rolling of thunder, when it occurs with less intensity, with the rattling of many carts, travelling hastily over bumpy cobblestones.... In Peru the intensity of this curious clamour appears to correlate directly with the intensity of the quake that follows; the same is said in Calabria, where they call this dreaded phenomenon *il rombo*.'
— Friedrich Hoffmann, *A History of Geognosy and an Account of Volcanic Phenomena* (1838)

LANDSCAPE

All around: a dwindling moraine landscape. Soft hills, fields, peat moss bogs in outlying depressions, karst protuberances with oak groves, chestnut trees, blades of grass sharp and thin, growing on ridges less mountainous than they appear, which nevertheless offer a view: over the hill country, the crests dotted with churches and villages, here and there a castle-like ruin that is in reality a mouldering vestige of the First World War. For its mellifluousness the landscape has a tremendous material shift to thank; glaciers, boulders, matter that it carried all the way here with an inevitable clamour that far exceeded the rumble of a *rombo*. Not a *preluding roar*, as it was referred to, two hundred years ago, but rather an ongoing rage that no human ear could have endured.

To the south the hills surrender to flatland, to the magnitude of the sky, the openness of the sea. Giant cornfields, industrial strips, highways, gravel quarries at the rivers emptying into the Adriatic Sea. Piave, Tagliamento, Isonzo, each river carrying off its part of the Alps, dolomite metamorphic rocks, pre-alpine conglomerates, the Isonzo's karstic limestone, whose dazzling white colour people still attribute to the many bones of the soldiers fallen in the Battles of Isonzo. On clear days one can see from the hillcrests all the way to the sea, to the Grado Lagoon with dabs of island bushes, to the chiselled hotels of resort towns, like sharp, uneven teeth on the horizon.

The river that defines this hilly region is the Tagliamento. A wild river, as they say. Yet, aside from the few weeks of high water from snow melt and torrential downpours, the wild thing about it is rather the emptiness, the vastness of the unregulated stone bed, the caprice of the sparse rivulets, always seeking out new paths and courses. At the point where it exits the mountains and

8

enters the moraine landscape, the river changes course, abandoning its eastward path and veering south, taking along with it the Fella from the north – hesitantly, both wavering, turquoise and white; a wavering that produced a giant triangular field of pebbles and scree, which separates the Carnic Alps from the Julian Alps, a bright plane like a wound, a space of procrastination before a backdrop of mountain valleys, before the secluded zones with their own languages, dulled by waning use, their own shrill, helpless songs and tricky dances.

The cemeteries of the hill country villages all have their own small, secluded summits with little churches and a view to the north, to the mountains, the trench of the Tagliamento valley, the narrow passage of the Fella valley, which the Romans passed through, heading north, and the Celts, heading south. To the northwest lie the Carnic Alps, cleft peaks behind pre-Alpine mountain chains, a picture book of the violence that certainly transpired in order for these mountains to be formed. The picture book is located precisely at the unstable point where two lithospheric plates collide, uneasy about their positions. Their discontent radiates eastward, into the mountain valleys of Italia Slava and the mellifluous hill country north of the coastal strip.

To the northeast one's gaze is met by the Julian Alps and the Alps, the defensive wall of Monte Musi, appearing grey, blue, violet or orange, depending on the light and clarity. The cliffs are sheer in any light: a dark barrier, unclimbable, insurmountable, at the eastern end a mountain peak arching over it, that is, Monte Canin, white from chalk or snow, the dull eye tooth, the border tooth of the valley behind.

Two zones meet before the mountains, continental and Mediterranean climates, the winds, precipitations and temperatures of two migratory fields, to the land and to the sea. Thunderstorms, gales, deluges, earthquakes that all tirelessly abrade the traces of human migration running through this region that – no matter how worn down they may become – still never allow themselves to be erased. The sky falls into a dark mood, the *rombo* is never far away.

QUAKE

The earthquake is everywhere. In the rubble of collapsed houses overgrown by ivy on Statale 13, in the cracks and scars on the large buildings, in the shattered gravestones, in the crookedness of reconstructed cathedrals, in the empty lanes of the old villages, interconnected like honeycomb, in the ugly new houses and developments modelled on the dream location of suburbia found in American television series. The new houses stand out in the open on the field, at a distance from the rattled towns, often with only a single story – here the main point being to minimize the material that might fall on one's head, in case once again there is... as there was *that* year, the earthquake year of 1976. Now it's half a lifetime ago or more, but the script it inscribed in everyone's memories has not faded: it is forever being notched anew by the act of recollection, by speaking of all the wheres and hows, of searching for shelter and the fear and listening out for further rumblings – in garages, in the open air, squeezed into the family Fiat, buried beneath rubble, among the dead, a cat in one's arm. If one laid them out, all these evoked images would stretch from here, the cemetery with a view to the north, all the way to the harshly hatched line of Monte Musi, purple-blue in the distance, more a peak-of-muzzle-and-snout than a mountain of muses, jags around the muzzle for the eye tooth Monte Canin. Everything spelled in the language of the mountains. Perhaps at the end there would be an unexpected trail leading up to its ridge, from where one could look down onto the valley at the foot of Monte Canin, a small river valley which would form a right angle with the path of evoked images from the earthquake. One would hope for doldrums on such a day in order to read the images, for a celebratory calm to walk in along the path of images.

But today it is windy. Right by the wall with a view to the mountains that look as if folded together in this light without shadow, beside a grave sealed by a layer of cement smooth and white with a faded wreath of plastic flowers on it, stands a short man with white hair and bad teeth, talking into his phone. He is describing the grave, emphasizing that it is clean and orderly, and he slowly pronounces the name on it, even mentioning the wreath – on the fadedness of the flowers, however, he does not comment – and in conclusion, as if responding to the voice at the other end of the line, he says: Memory is an animal, it barks with many mouths.

ANSELMO

The short man with white hair and bad teeth is named Anselmo. He is a council worker who always requests work at the cemetery. There is a lot to do there the layer of dirt, covering the mound of rock is thin, and the number of graves limited. The columbaria have to be expanded, graves need to be levelled, remains brought into the ossuary, trees pruned and cut down, the stability of the grave plaques and stones tested. Anselmo knows his way around. He is familiar with the locations where the graves are sinking, knows what kind of damage gravestones can

11

incur and which cemetery plot would be safest in case of an earthquake. He advises against mausoleums, pointing to the cracks in the walls of the showy family burial units. He banters with grave visitors and offers himself up as a confidant to bereaved persons visiting from out of town.

The cemetery is a recommended stop for hikers and cyclists passing through: on the northwest side of the wall there is a long panorama board where one can read the name of every peak. There the semicircle formed by the peaks and crests, surrounding the moraine landscape as if holding it in a rescuing embrace – on the west, north, and east – stretches out like a straight chain before the beholder, who first has to get used to the distortion of the landscape, letting their gaze wander back and forth between the image and the mountain range, while they graze with their fingertips the peaks on the panorama board, as if they could thus feel their constitution. Anselmo is wont to approach these day-trippers, as well, and tell them about the landscape. He always directs their gaze to Monte Canin and its summit, covered in snow into spring, and mentions that he grew up in the shadow of this mountain. When the peak is hidden behind clouds, Anselmo says: It doesn't want to show itself today. A moody one, that Canin.

6 MAY
On the morning of 6 May a rosy light falls on the snow clinging to Monte Canin's peak. It soon fades, the sun lies low. The slopes are quiet in the valley on this morning in early May, chalk white and green from beeches and hazelnut bushes, metallic grey from silverberry at the riverside. Beneath thin clouds the heat disperses.

—

Olga leaves the house early, heading down the road to the bus. When asked later, she will say: That morning as I walked down the steps to the road I saw a snake, a *carbon*, the kind you usually find down below along the river, and not up in the village. It lay on a piece of the wall, as if to sun itself, a black stick, yet the sun wasn't shining, although it was warm. The cuckoo was calling ceaselessly, already in the morning. The cuckoo and this snake and all the stories I'd ever heard about this kind of snake came to my mind then, all this I can remember very well.

—

In the afternoon Anselmo helps scythe. It is still early in the year to be cutting. He will remember that Thursday. I still remember it exactly, he will say. We got out of school early on Thursdays. I still remember that it was hot outside, and after lunch my sister and I had to help down below, in the valley on the hillside, with the first mowing. The grass was already high.

The sun is a lurid hole in the clouds that day, it burns the children's necks until they hurt. The crickets chat thinly, hastily, as if they have somewhere to be. Their grandmother cuts the grass with a scythe. The grass is heavy, she sweats, and the scythe becomes dull again and again, more often than usual, and the blade has to be whetted. The children hurry with their raking and piling. Get it done already! one can hear the grandmother calling out again and again, Do it faster!

Anselmo will remember that she was angry at the children for being slow, but she is also angry at the grass, which appears so dry and bristly and yet dulls the scythe, as if it were wet. The whetting stone strikes the blade without an echo, as if the air had swallowed the sound. That whole time, Anselmo will later report, we heard our neighbour's greenfinch all the way down in the meadow.

It's screaming as if there were a fire, says the man mowing the meadow lot next to theirs. He swings his scythe back broadly and drives it into the blades, and the sweet grass sinks down onto the earth. Still he has to pause and whet the blade just as often as Anselmo's grandmother.

—

On 6 May snow on the peak shimmers into the shadowless morning light. The smallest mechanical action would be enough to cause the snow fields to slide into the valley. An imprudent hiker, falling rocks – that would already be enough. But this time of year there is no one out in the mountains.

—

The snake that Olga sees on the wall in the morning is black as coal. It loves dampness. It lives in water and on land and is not poisonous. In the spring when they mate, the male and female snakes entwine, as if to form a coiled rope. If they fear being interrupted, they close themselves off, thus coiled, forming a ring that can transfer an electric shock if touched from the outside. After mating, the two *carbon* snakes remain together until death do them part.

—

Lina is nervous this morning. The siskin calls out wretchedly. Her brother is looking for a job, and she knows he won't find one. But something else remains in her memory.

What I still remember about 6 May, she later begins one day, as if writing an essay for school: Because it had been so warm, on that day we were already mounding up the soil on the potato plants, that is certain. We heard sparrow hawks, their brief, tight tones calling out to one another, we talked about it. There were three of us in the field. My brother was back from living abroad. He always liked to tell us scary stories. On that day it was a snake that someone had driven over, by the village entrance. He saw it. If it was a female snake and had not yet laid its eggs, it will bring bad luck, he said. Then the male snakes will slither through the village, searching for the guilty person. Must have been the bus driver, he said. I know the bus driver now, I also knew him then. He didn't live in our village. After his afternoon drive he always parked outside the cemetery, where he enjoyed his lunch. As my brother told his story, I wondered whether a snake would be capable of finding the bus driver. While we worked, a sudden gust of cold wind came, very brief. The wind comes from the snow, still lying up there, my brother said. The snow and this heat, they don't go together.

—

On 6 May a thin white layer of clouds blankets the sky, causing the beams of sunlight to become particularly sharp, broken frequently as they are by tiny drops of steam. In the afternoon a peculiar phenomenon occurs. In a doubled reflection, two pale suns briefly grace the sky directly above the snowy peak of Canin, standing eye to eye with the sun, which glides in mist over the valley. The double sun soon dissipates.

—

In the meadows are already spurges, knapweeds, campions; on the waysides is blue bugle. And pale pink catchflies. Here they call it *sclopit*. The bloom consists mainly of a two-part bladder. Children pick the blossoms and crush them in their balled-up fists, letting them explode in two brief cracks. It sounds like *sclo-pit*. The flower is named after the sound of the blooms bursting. The leaves of *sclopit* are harvested before the flowers. They are pointy and narrow and of a pale, somewhat dull green colour. Everyone has their own *sclopit* spot. Some people divulge theirs, others keep it for themselves.

Mara gathers *sclopit* on 6 May. Before she goes out, she has to lock in her mother, who has already half-forgotten the world. She had always acquiesced calmly, but that morning she cries out from behind the locked door, as if it were a matter of life and death. Mara walks uphill, away from the cries. When later the conversation turns to 6 May, she does not mention her cries: I reached a meadow at the edge of the forest above a steep slope, where the *sclopit* was everywhere, not a blossom yet in sight, she says. Jays called out among the pines. I filled my cloth, until I could hardly tie it shut. When I arrived home, the *sclopit* was wilted and droopy, as if someone had sat on it. It smelled like cut grass. I heard a child cry out and was startled. So came the evening.

—

In the afternoon on 6 May the sky above the mountain ridge turns grey-blue and dark in the southwest, as if a storm were coming from that direction, as rarely occurs.

16

This pseudo-wall of clouds remains motionless for a while, then dissipates, and the sun rests white and lurid and large in the sky. Below it the snow plane facing the valley lies as if submerged in a tempestuous yellow.

—

At night in front of their doors some people place hollowed out slabs of wood filled with milk for the black snakes. In the morning the bowl is always empty, so they say. It brings luck. The *carbon* is a clever snake. One story goes like this: Once a sparrow hawk snatched up a *carbon*. In its talons the bird carried it back to its nest. Before the bird knew what had happened, the young snake had devoured all the eggs in the nest. I'll return them to you if you bring me back, said the snake. The sparrow hawk promised, and the snake spewed out the eggs. Then the sparrow hawk brought back the snake, and since then in the valley sparrow hawks no longer snatch up snakes.

—

In the valley some people keep goats, while other people, who have more money, keep a cow or two. The stalls are not large. Gigi's family had always kept goats. I only know about two things, Gigi says. Wood and goats. I know how to fell timber. I know how to milk a goat.

On 6 May in the afternoon he comes home from his work in the forest. The sun burns, without shining. He passes by the cemetery, where there is not a shadow, and sweats. On the street he sees a runover snake. It lies there, black in a spot of blood. Flies rest on the blood. From the edge of the forest the cuckoo calls. Gigi still remembers that the goats were stubborn. Their fur felt sticky. It was hot. On days like this, one wondered when Canin would finally shed its snow. When I was finished with the first goat, the second one didn't want to come, he remembers. That had never happened before. It stood crookedly behind the pushcart. Behind the cart, its head and legs seemed mismatched. Nearby a bird in a cage whistled so loudly the milk might have turned sour. All the dogs in the village were barking. When I finished milking, both goats wanted to stand behind the pushcart. They stood there, incredibly still. It was already turning dark. The milk smelled bitter.

—

In the late afternoon on 6 May a dark shadow falls over Canin's peak and the remaining snow fields, resting on them, like a hand. A short burst of cold wind, and the shadow disappears, as if the hand were pulled away.

—

Why should I remember? Toni says. Why not forget it all instead? Come on, Toni, tell us something, people say, we all know something about 6 May. All right, Toni says:

On Fridays my mother smoked cheese. The evening before I always had to gather wood, so that in the morning everything would be ready in the smokehouse. That evening I didn't want to gather wood. I can't remember why. I sat on the veranda and whittled something. Go get wood, my father said, but I remained there, seated. Below on the street people headed home. Someone whistled a tune, I think. All the dogs in the neighbourhood were howling. My father smacked me on the back of my head. I took the basket and went down to the woodshed. It wasn't a proper shed, more like a few posts and shelves with a roof on top. The back wall was the side of a hill. Dirt and stone. It wasn't late. Still light out. I took a log from the pile, and a snake shot out of the crack, between the woodpile and the hillside. It was black and long and must have been thick as my arm. After all, I was practically still a child. The grass rustled below the snake, which disappeared down towards the river. I ran back up to the house and yelled, I just saw a huge snake. I don't believe you, my father said. I had to go back down alone for the wood and carry up the basket, all the while listening out for every sound. Everything was eerie to me, even the voices from below on the road, the yowling of the dogs, the bird calls.

—

Before dusk falls on 6 May the bare cliff on the south side of the peak lies bathed in an orange-red hue, as if reflecting the light of a sun, setting on the invisible western horizon. Briefly this glow reflects onto the snow fields, which are already in the process of sinking into the evening shadows.

—

The birds in the trees are restless. Silvia stands at the village exit, waiting for her father. She strains to hear the sound of a motor. But she hears only the brief, excited, flat trills of the birds in the trees. Like a rattling. How the birds rattled, she will say.

The sky is heavy. The mountains to the west are indistinct. Like shadows.

My father had promised to come home on a moped, Silvia says. He peddled off on the knife grinder's bicycle, with our neighbour. That was weeks ago already. Then he wrote a letter, I'll be back on 6 May. I still remember it exactly. He had got a job at the factory and would buy himself the moped, he wrote. I listened and listened into the valley. Then I saw him coming. He looked so small, and I could see that he was limping, and he was pushing the moped. I walked towards him, jumping over a crack in the street. Not until I was mid-air did I realize it was a snake. Run over. So not a snake any more, not really. Snake mush. I walked over to my father, I was so happy he had arrived. I was spooked out there, all alone outside the village, it was already turning evening.

Silvia's father is very tired. He lifts her up in the air and sets her down on the moped's saddle. The fuel ran out. Someone had a bad day, he says, as they pass by the flattened snake. At least that's how Silvia will tell of it later.

—

Occasionally the *carbon* is seized by fury: then it bites its own tail and stiffens into a ring, charged with electricity. In this form it throws itself into motion, and the rolling ring quickly picks up speed and races forward with a high-pitched buzzing and hissing, until it's derailed by some obstacle, at which point the electricity is discharged and the jaws release the tip of the tail. The snake lies weary, as if from an incredible exertion, and is hardly able to take cover and seek shelter. In this weary state after the race the snake is open to attack.

—

Anselmo has to go to bed early, school is in session. It's not dark out yet, a yellow gloaming. There are no swifts to be heard; usually at dusk they overtake the roofs and the church tower. But in the yard the dog wails, as if someone were kicking it. The musicians are arriving at Anselmo's neighbour's house, to rehearse. This is what Anselmo remembers: They tuned and tuned before playing a few bars, then cursed and tuned their instruments again, but before long the bass was back out of tune, or one of the fiddles, and the musicians cursed and argued, and then a bow glided over the strings of the bass, and then over the strings of the first and then the second fiddle, and the bass again, in this manner in a circle and back and forth, the canary in the cage at the house below near the path whistled and whistled as if it were a matter of life and death, so loud that the musicians complained about it, too, and from time to time it was utterly silent, near dark and silent like never before, a very deep kind of silence that came on all of a sudden, and then a deep drone started, and a rumbling and a trembling and a grinding coursed through everything, and I jumped up and looked out the window, where I saw, in the last light of dusk, the dark snow come loose from Canin.

SISMA
On the evening of 6 May an earthquake shakes the region. The ground opens up, houses collapse, people and animals are buried beneath the rubble, the clocks on the church towers stand still, it is nine o'clock, black snakes are fleeing into the river, below the peak of Monte Canin a cloud of snow travels through the evening into the valley.

The earthquake is the result of tectonic plates shifting. There are countless words to explain what transpired at the end of a day of three suns, yowling dogs, restless *carbon* snakes, shrill birds. Words like tectonic plate boundaries,

21

spreading centre, lithosphere. Beautiful words that you can hold in your hand like small foreign petrified life forms: Hypocentre. Surface rupture. Earthquake lights. Rupture velocity. The tremor's path. An earthquake modifies the surface of the planet, it is said. It can be measured. The magnitude of the earthquake on 6 May was not even that great, according to the units of the man-made scale. 'The assessment relates to the physical body and overlooks the fact that the planet may well be measured by man, but not in relation to him,' is written in a book. In any case: The world is not the same.

Tremors seized parts of the Earth's crust, rattling everything far and wide. *Dislocations* occurred, and all the frightened survivors were unavoidably reminded that they live in a *zone of disruption*, and without going so far as to examine the landscape for hinge lines and fractures, fault lines and radial cracks, without consciously knowing what a 'mine tailing landscape at the edge of a subsidence area' means, they nevertheless understand, even if only by the streaks of mortar and mites of stone in their hair, that what they have just experienced cannot be erased or redeemed, because it is beyond the categories of good and evil.

DISTURBANCES
What did the land look like before? One forgets all at once, and over the years will continue to search for it in dreams – what did the ground look like before the crack, before the fragments, the rubble and the grinding marks, the ground beneath one's feet, from one day to the next?

The ground of daily life becomes a disturbed terrain, where everyone searches for what they have lost: groping, looking, listening out.

22

Meanwhile, at the foot of Canin, in the beech-lined low grounds the limekilns stand firm, where they once fired the white stones from the beds of brooks and rivers, a tedious work that is all but forgotten today: gathering the limestone and firing it, abiding by the limekiln and covering the stone with clay. Wood and lime: two fruits of a barren land, all memory driven out of them in the act of securing a living. Sites where fire briefly rules over a stone shaped by water.

MONTE SAN SIMEONE

At the point where the Fella and Tagliamento rivers meet, near Venzone, Monte San Simeone ascends: a high, conical mountain with a forested back and a rocky face. In the rambling, varying, forever trembling stories about the earthquake, the *rombo* is said to have originated here. Below, or *inside* of it, as the current narrative would have it, the Orcolat once rumbled, the monstrous earthquake of 1976. A mythical creature whose traces can never be erased.

The peak of Monte San Simeone can be climbed from two sides: the steep, rocky side of the river confluence, or the gentler way, up the many serpentine curves on the side of deep blue Lago di Cavazzo, the icy lake left behind in the former Tagliamento riverbed. One can only speculate as to why the river changed course; nothing appears to have shifted and blocked its way. Call it a mood swing. Drawn to the other river, to the other valley, to other rocks, towards the east. Rivers have their own reasons. Even now, centuries later, the deserted beds, long conquered by settlement, draw attention to themselves on autumn and winter mornings with some thin mist, some impalpable trace.

Monte San Simeone, and all the monstrosity attributed to it, is framed by the Tagliamento riverbeds: the old one, the new one, and the one that joins the Fella. From above, to the west one looks down onto the placid lake, and to the northeast onto the large, pebbly triangle formed at the confluence. And one sees each river's colour, the Tagliamento, white despite many darker stones, and the Fella, turquoise despite the limestone's blazing white. Both rivers flow to the south in a single bed, yet they do not mix; they remain side by side, turquoise and white, until the colours peter out under the light and are only blindingly reflective, a web of streams in an ever-expanding gravel bed that separates the eastern and western sides of the Tagliamento.

From the eastern side of Monte San Simeone one looks onto Venzone, the reconstructed cathedral, beside it the untouched ruins of a white stone church. One looks onto the overgrown earthquake remains of small towns near the mountain and alongside the river, and the new settlements of uniform houses on ground presumed more solid. This is where the mountains recede. The moraine hills flatten out into the plains, stretching all the way to the sea. Here, at Monte San Simeone, one could draw a line, dividing the light into two kinds: the sharp, richly shadowed blue light of the mountains, and the soft, vibrating, shadow-poor light of the plains. A twofold land of passage. Countless people marched through here, brought things and took others, learned, kept moving. Gold takers and glass bringers, those hungry for war and those weary of war, those disabled by war. Tired seekers of the right place, who followed the green woodpecker's call and ultimately named themselves after the bird, as if by doing so they might shed whatever foreignness clung to them, as if they could thus conjure a homeland, a repository for all their stories, from their legendary departure down to their legendary sedentariness. Multitudes were flushed into the valleys by the woes of one era or another; they climbed uphill, the river always on their minds, the river that had made the valley its own, that they did not want to let fade from their memories. By following the river it was always possible to find a way out of the valley, should the need arise. They learned to live, to outlive, to live on; they conferred a name to all they saw, in their languages from elsewhere, and they sang, as one does, their songs in the name of that Elsewhere, in languages that otherwise wasted away in isolation and, aside from song, were suitable only for confirming their state of affairs: driven off course, in a valley alongside a river. Languages suited to naming an *us* in a landscape favourably disposed to no one, which behaved according to laws that no one could ever grow old enough to understand. Avalanches, boggy brooks, moors, every discord and displacement accompanied by a deep, trembling sigh. A material sigh, without melancholy.

STRADA STATALE 13

Statale 13 – la Pontebbana, as it was once called, back when it was narrower, bumpier – is 222 kilometres long and runs from Tarvisio to Venice. It passes through the Val Canale, following the course of the former Via Iulia, the Roman road that brought trade, migration and conquests. Advances into the foreign from both sides, north and south; in the mountainous region it leads through a valley at times cramped, at times mellifluous, a road of natural resources with labyrinthine turn-offs into treasure hunters' terrain. North of the spot that went down as the earthquake's epicentre, the state road runs in the shadow of a highway, built after the earthquake, which dissects the towns that were once well-disposed to all travellers and embedded into the landscape, cutting them off from the migration that nurtured and nourished the valley for so long, and through so many tremors.

At the confluence of the Fella and Tagliamento rivers, Statale 13 leaves the mountains for the mild rolling hills. It is a transit road, a bustling trucker's stretch, marked by black brake skids on the roadway and crosses on the crash barriers, dusty plastic flowers twined around them in remembrance of driving casualties. Shacks stand at a discreet distance from the road, their parking spaces large, like those outside a factory. Souvenir shops with amphorae, concrete angels and garden gnomes for tourists heading home back north, motels, restaurants in the shadow of receding slopes with a view to the no-man's-land strips separating the road from the riverbank. Trucks crowd the parking lot of a pink motel. The motel has a bombastic name featuring an English word, spelled incorrectly. Next to the motel is a small petrol station with a luncheonette; the petrol station attendant is also the cook. People take their lunch there, sometimes having to stand in line; there is always a dish of the day, water and wine. When a car pulls in to fill up, lunch service is interrupted, but this doesn't happen very often. The woman is tall and thin and wears her hair, streaked by grey, twisted at the nape of her neck. Her name is Silvia. Once the luncheonette customers have all left, she takes her lunch standing, leaning against the door, a bowl in her hand. She squints in the sunlight. Traffic rolls past on the street. Some truckers beep their horns. She always wears a dress, polka-dotted, striped, flowered – faded clothing of a bygone era. If it weren't for her dress and the pink motel, this entire section of the state road could be taken for the set of a black-and-white film. Nearly every day a delivery truck full of rubble stops at the gas station. The driver exits the vehicle, sometimes he gets petrol, he never eats. Occasionally he places himself directly before the woman, balancing a hand on the frame of the door that she leans on while eating, the way men in old films often place themselves in front of a woman and look down at her. Do you always eat standing up? he might ask. The woman merely shrugs her shoulders. She doesn't answer his question, doesn't suggest he come in and take a look at the old suits of a former lover – be he deceased, withered, or dropped – that might be piling up in the back room of her quarters. She carries the dishes over to the sink and gets to work, stopping only when a customer pulls up. The driver climbs back in and heads off, northbound. He is headed to the drop-off location for construction waste, also on Statale 13. This is his occupation. He is paid to collect construction rubble throughout the entire region and bring it to the drop-off location, which, according to the sign on the gate, is already full up on concrete waste and cannot accept any more everlasting scrap. Everything is covered in a thick dust, as if emitted by the rubble. A few men in dirty overalls always loiter around the unshapely fragments, waiting for acquaintances who pay for permission to unload behind the breakroom sheds, sign notwithstanding. The overall-clad men rearrange the smaller pieces and restack piles of balanced toilets, sinks, bidets and bathtubs. *Inerti* is the elegant name for this rubble; it does not stir, already familiar with the lethargy of eternity. It will not decompose in any period of time measurable in human terms, but will simply remain as it is, whiling away its life expectancy vastly superior to that of humans, becoming at most overgrown with moss, offering up its coarse pores and cracks to undemanding creeping plants. The rubble driver is amicable with the men in overalls, who wave to greet him, Toni is his name, a welcome guest. They clear out the back of the delivery truck, dust rising into the air as the rubble falls to the ground, and after they've finished unloading the men drink a beer. If the sun doesn't burn too hot they take their beer outside, sitting down on a concrete block that almost looks like a bench and, forever smoothed by the men's tired backsides, has neither creeping plants nor moss growing on it. If it rains or is too hot, they drink inside, in the shack with blind glass panes facing the road. Ascending behind the rubble yard is a rocky acclivity, not very high, yet steep, and notched on one side where a rockslide was set loose by the earthquake. The boulders that slipped down now lie in a pile on the meagre ground, where sheep once grazed; it is said that the rockslide struck the animals and shepherd dead, buried a hut. Stories and rumours like this one have lined the state road since the earthquake, covering its traces like a creeping vine, a bare whisper that can be wiped away with an arm motion, beer bottle held tightly in the raised hand, just like that.

BED

For a short distance Statale 13 runs parallel to the Tagliamento, which has already swallowed the Fella. More than anything else, this river is a bed, a landscape of stone that changes with the water's rise and fall and flow and trickle, a border land that builds its islands and then levels them, sowing thin-trunked willows only to rip them back out, washing away its banks and eroding them, building them up and then turning its back on them, until they sink as flat tongues and bleed into the water, as if searching for a new form. The bed digests its own history of the wars and the ringing names, with all those drowned, those killed in action, the fallen horses and broken carriages and lost treasures and surrendered weapons, with bones and bullets and splinters and helmets and skulls.

Among the boulders, pebbles and shards of glass washed milky and smooth are variously sized concrete fragments that stand tilted, defying the water in a different way than the leftover solid and stony things which gradually submit to the currents and learn to want to reach the sea. The concrete fragments are rigid and inflexible, positioning themselves against any current. They distinguish themselves from the meticulously smooth stones with implicit drawings and lines and veins of a different nature, and seek the edges, the banks, the coves set apart from the current, where they come into their own as wreckage, maintain their fragmented nature and remain witness: earthquake breakage, remains of house and farm and charge, things carted away that do not submit to anything new. A young addition to the old river: the earthquake rubble.

VOICES

On the state road, not far from the turn-off into the valley, an elderly woman tends a small stall with a pointy gable roof and decals emulating wood carvings in alpine style; 'generic alpine', say the gable and carvings, but the presentation is further specified by small Italian flags rustling in the wind. A last stop before the final leg to the border, in the shade of highway stilts. Bright red lipstick crumbles in the corners of the woman's mouth, and when the wind blows through her carefully arranged hair, she immediately smooths it with her hand. Her hair is dyed a coppery colour, a piercing shade in this peculiar light between mountains moving together. Below a corrugated plastic roof, dangling from the crossbeams of her small stand are bunches of garlic, rustling, dry and old. There are embroidered napkins for sale, as well as carved roots, pebbles with miniature paintings of Alpine glow and shepherds with goats. Postcards. In a cardboard box at the edge of the table are a few CDs. The cover art is inserted aslant, printed carelessly in bright colours, homemade. The various images depict a choir with snow-covered Monte Canin in the background, two musicians holding the local instruments – a violin known as the *zitira* and the *bunkula*, a type of bass – before the backdrop of Monte Canin in a bonnet of snow, and an exposed bell, hanging from a crooked frame in a broken tower – this, too, before the backdrop of the snow-covered mountain. There are no words, the images should speak for themselves, although the woman cannot possibly expect any locals to shop here. At best she can hope for expats, people who have left this place to escape the hardship, the narrowness, the poverty and lack of prospects, people who return now and then, in order to puncture the uncomfortable bubble they carry around inside them, which fills up again and again with the seepage of an indistinct longing: perhaps it will burst in a bar, at the cemetery, in a narrow lane. On a box of several CDs only the mountain is shown. *Rombo* is written on it. And: *25 anni dopo. Le voci del terremoto*. Voices of the earthquake.

A few young people hang around behind a closed buffet shack, smoking. A tourist bus whooshes past. During a pause in the traffic, a green woodpecker calling out from the forested hillside. And from very far away, an oriole.

The woman named Olga closes her stand at evening. A shutter pulls down and is secured in front of the sales window. She locks the door on the back wall of the stand and carries her bag and the box of CDs over to her old, dull-red Fiat Uno and drives off, southbound, along the river.

VALLEY

Shortly after the confluence of the Fella and Tagliamento rivers, after the mountains have moved together to form a defensive wall in front of the hill country vista, a narrow road turns off Statale 13. The road marking the way into the valley is inconspicuous, and the road itself appears indecisive, winding through an ugly village of modern houses with dull shimmering aluminium window frames, and ultimately leaving behind on its right the road into the valley, in order to turn back to Statale 13. No venture into remote territory. Squeezed between the Fella, the highway, and the steep limestone mountains, there is something random about this place. Transit, barracked soldiers and bitumen were their bread and butter here, but the bitumen has since run dry or been plugged up and the mine is a sight in the mountains that no one asks to see, no matter how good of a black story it makes against the white rocks of the valley that is petering out. The workers who marched in long rows up to the higher-lying mine and returned, smeared black, to the village after their shift – from time to time carrying down an injured worker on a hastily cobbled-together stretcher – these workers are *bergfertig*, as they say, *mountain spent*; they toiled to death and were then done away with, and if anything now roam about as spirits, so that superstition may never die and they, the workers, will not be entirely forgotten. Whoever searches for work goes away – this has already been the case for decades; they go abroad, to other mines, to build roads, to the industrial zones further in the West. The soldiers are still here, these loitering young men who fill the bars along the state road and slog through the mountains with heavy heads, completing drills; once tourist season is over, they sit with the hungry eyes of children at long tables in the highway restaurants, where behind the alpine décor in the kitchen are stacked boxes of pale, grey-pink pieces of poultry, each piece waiting to be routinely processed into a portion of grilled chicken by the deliberate hand movements of a line cook.

But coming back to that narrow, easily overseen turn-off before what few shops the village has to offer. It leads up into the valley, into outlying land, far off from transit routes, into the rugged territory, rocky terrain. First it travels over another confluence, a smaller version of the Tagliamento-Fella triangle, a broad, blazing field of gravel with thin rivulets, white and green; a ubiquitous rush, greater than anything the visible water is capable of producing. At the foot of a mountain, at the end of the steep way down, rivers and streams are wont to relocate beneath the surface, beneath gravel and pebbles, undermining one's perception with their rush, their invisibility, only to rise back to the surface once the mountains are behind them. A camouflage manoeuvre, to avoid being held up.

The valley is a world in itself. From within there is no view to the outside, unless one were to follow the road out, scale a mountain, far exceed all limits of quotidian performance in order to look to the hill country blurred by mist, and the plain shimmering out to the horizon, the subsidence field extending to the sea.

Four, five villages, all scattered, with views of cliffs, forests, rivers. The terrain is accessible. Traversed and beribboned by bumpy paths and trails – following streams, following the river, along agricultural stretches. Here livestock was once driven to pasture, limestone brought for firing, felled timber taken into the valley. A network of traces runs through the forests and across the stony fields, leading around ravines and searching out fords. Paths of duty, paths of desire, paths of flight, some concealed by pillows of heather, distorted by severe weather, broken open by roots. Interventions by nature, a force that seems to be well-disposed yet. Newborns were brought to baptism in padded panniers, in long funeral processions coffins were carried slowly over forest paths to the only cemetery in the valley, cheese was brought in; there were deserters, off-season hunters, partisans sent on a safe path into the thicket, across a border, to a shelter undetectable to those not familiar with it. Everyone in the valley would have said about at least one path: I could walk it in my sleep. There I know what to expect, what's lurking, what sustains. But the earthquake subverted this accessibility and dashed all certainty about the paths. Fallen rocks, mudslides, diverted waterways, dammed lakes and ravaged forests disrupted the paths, changing their courses, even their destinations. Sparse terrain, as they say. No more sleepwalking. A time to learn, wide-awake, about the new situation, the new order of things. The old stopping places and mountain locations became the stuff of legends, thrust offside, then left untouched. The sparse traces left by those gone lost, which the clueless bereaved had read continuously, were wiped away or displaced. Uncertainty spread. Doubt about what belonged to which cardinal direction, which view, the sun's path. New routes were trampled, as if in determined defiance to the obliteration of the familiar, and the confusion that that entailed. The new paths acquiesced to the terrain, levelled off, became a transcription of that intervention, became a sign for the renewed accessibility.

At the midpoint of the lower valley, the river is dammed. The dam isn't very high, just high enough that youths can place themselves behind the curtain of water and lean in, or dare advance and then fall, pulling in others along with them; in rainy summers an eddying pool forms near the dam, the water mountain-cold and pale green. The river describes an arch. Between the rising hillside and the bank is a space for cars, tents, two or three trailers that remain parked there all year round, surrounded by improvised attachments made from lumber, tarps and poles, alongside a wooden hut, declared a buffet. A crooked, shuttered kiosk bears a label in the local language, still spoken by a few hundred people. Perhaps there are souvenirs tucked away behind the shutter. Or in busier times the kiosk functions as an information desk with a specialist available to take questions and share news of people who stayed in the villages. Deaths, births, weddings, accidents. Events of all kinds. Whether it's souvenirs or news, this service applies only to those stealthy fleeting visitors who return to the homeland they shed like dead skin, yet dare not travel any further into the valley, to the villages, uphill, lest they become caught in the snares of memory and sentiment.

The earthquake doled out its traces unevenly; one or two villages were rebuilt entirely, while others appear only to have been mended. The last village on the road, high at the end of the upper valley, still lies mostly in shambles. High red dahlias grow beside a fence; someone planted them and in winter must stow them away: it certainly gets cold here. From the dahlia fence, Canin is visible. Past the lean meadows, the small clump of Scotch pines, outcroppings of sheer rock; from a distance it appears as if not a single plant could find a hold here, not even moss. Two tiny figures, also in red, cross a snow field. Or is it bare limestone? White rocks – grooved, ribbed – false snow with a brief memory.

GRADES OF DISRUPTION

It is said that animals are much quicker to sense the vibrations that gradually build up in the Earth's interior and eventually exceed the stress limit in the spreading centre, causing the tectonic plates to snag and tip, irrevocably shifting the order of hollow cavities and mass, the order of emptiness and fullness.

A human being, with two legs planted on the ground, with scythe, hammer, saw, wood and fiddle, becomes the most clueless creature of all, once the vibrations can no longer be overheard.

Olga wonders if the *carbon* – its entire body arrested to the ground – has a particular feel for the early phases of the quake; whether the snake, lying on the wall in the early morning, was listening to some processes deep in the earth, or perhaps even should have served as a warning to passers-by; whether the run-over snake, utterly lost in anticipation of the tremors, was able to forget the dangers of the immediate world; whether the bus driver knew what he had wrought; whether the bus driver really was responsible for this unforgettable and, as it appeared on the day of the event, unredeemable defilement of the road, now suddenly erased and suppressed, overwritten by the crack.

—

And the birds? How can one explain their disquiet? They who do not touch the ground. Does the air vibrate? Is it the light? The odd shift from shadows and hazy light and the air's reflections, the brief little gusts that the birds pierce in pointed flight, or flutter around in in the white light – are these all messages, communicating something to them?

To Toni, the drone – this deep, unfamiliar, tremendous rumble – seems to go on for minutes before the actual quake begins. His father thrusts him, his mother, his younger siblings onto the street. A piece of the neighbour's wooden balcony had broken off and slid down the hillside, along with the birdcage and greenfinch, whose shrill whistle of all afternoon and evening is now but a squawk. Toni feels his father's fist on his back: Go, get the farmer! he commands, and Toni is afraid. A beam breaks from the piece of fallen balcony roof, smothering the squawk.

—

The dogs' yelping mixes with the clanking and rattling of the chains they struggle to break free from. As if driven by a sense of urgency, here and there someone bends down to let their dog off its chain before they drop their head into their hands in recognition of what has happened. The dogs do not run away, they understand nothing, attack no one, do not even chase one another or the stealthy, concealed cat; the dogs seek cover.

The air is full of sounds, from the distant thunder of the mountain faces to the trees groaning in the gardens and the wood bursting in the roofs, the shattering glass and the angry, dry rumble of stone. Human voices in a shrill state of agitation, taken to shelter, searching for neighbours, screaming from below the wreckage, clutching rubble, rolling, calling, sobbing, a wail in the dark.

—

Gigi gropes his way through wreckage and darkness, out to the goat shed. At the doorpost his hand brushes against something that feels like hair, sticky and moist. He climbs over fallen beams, hears no sound. Once his eyes have adjusted to the darkness he sees an outline of both goats. They stand behind the pushcart beside the intact wall. He runs his hand along their backs and feels their faint trembling, like an echo of the Earth's vibrations, not knowing where to go.

—

Boulders rolled into the valley, bowing watercourses. On their way down they felled aisles in the forest, bare earth now lies where woods once were; knapweeds, campions, catchflies, dandelions and bugle protrude along the avalanche tracks in the meadows; small blooming weeds have been ripped out at the roots, grey-silver field poplars and alders snapped at the banks' edges. Walls gape, roofs angle inward, doors protrude crookedly in this vast room where things are no longer in their right places.

—

Silvia stands beneath the archway to the yard and screams, her face hidden by her hands, small hands that her grandmother is now yanking at, they are solid as stone. Her grandmother's apron strings have come untied and dangle about her legs. Her hand is bleeding, a trace of blood smeared across the back of her hand. The moped is buried under the buckled shed. Only the back wheel sticks out, like a body part.

—

After the tremor a crack runs across the masonry wall of Mara's house on the side facing the yard, and the window is knocked out of its hinges. Mara, who since returning from gathering *sclopit* has heard her mother's cries and quiet whimpering, unlocks the bedroom door and guides out her mother, who, silent and smiling and dusted in white limestone debris, appears almost angelic.

—

Later everyone would talk about the sound. About the *rombo*. So it began. So everything changed, at a blow, as they say, although it was more of a collision, like the muffled, dull end of a motion rolled in from far away. Everyone committed this sound to memory under various names. Humming, whirring, roaring, murmuring, thundering, clattering, whooshing, rushing, rumbling, whistling, droning, blaring. And so on. Always dark, though. Even those who refer to it as a whistle emphasize how it whistled darkly. No one experienced it as screeching, piercing, or high-pitched. No one disagrees that it rose from the depths and did not, for instance, huff down the mountainside, even if a certain repetitive rumbling did follow – again and again on that first evening – once the shaken mountain mass came loose from the slope and descended into the valley.

—

Anselmo fumbles and pushes his way out behind his sister. His father roars, they should wait it out. Anselmo's hand brushes against the neck of his fiddle, jammed below the table beside the window, now completely warped. He extracts it and once outside he turns it this way and that, shaking the dust and mortar powder out of the hollow cavity, out of the body, still intact, after the quake's tremors have caused it to vibrate, perhaps as to save the entire fiddle.

—

In Lina's house the grey jug of wine broke, and her drunk brother cut his hand picking up a bulbous shard still swashing with wine.

TA LIPA POT

In the local Slavic language it means: the beautiful path.

Even if the way markers begin elsewhere, this trail commences as nearly all trails do: at an inn. The inn lies in the sun on the village outskirts, between the church and cemetery, on a kind of landscape gallery, a *balcone* with a view to the sparsely populated, rocky and wooded valley. Elderly men sit in the sun, drinking their morning wine. The inn has its own small grocery. A female salesclerk stocks the shelves, adjusts the position of a box on a side table collecting donations for foreign earthquake victims. Inside are four or five packets of cheap spaghetti, a pair of socks, a dishevelled Barbie doll, sugar.

On the counter are jars of garlic: green, white, chopped, whole cloves. On each jar a sticker reveals that the contents were prepared by Lina. Lina the garlic woman. Lina also runs the inn's kitchen. The menu is short. Polenta, potato cake, garlic soup, rabbit ragout, beans. While the men drink their morning wine, Lina stands at the rear kitchen door beside a stack of beverage crates, smoking. Her face is in the sun, her eyes are closed. Difficult to say her age. With her eyes closed, basking in the sun, entirely absorbed by the cigarette smoke caressing her larynx and airways, any question about the number of years she has accumulated is irrelevant. She is alive.

From the small lookout point in front of the restaurant, the beautiful path leads into a rocky hollow. From some height a thin stream falls between rocks marked by horizontal bands; grasses have established themselves along the bands, and between the grassy stripes the surface of the rocks is grey-black. On the front side of the depression the crumbly rock is a whitish yellow, like a glistening scab beside the smooth, layered blocks. On the upper edge of the rockfaces, a crown of alders, beeches, spruces, small oaks. Across the fresh, bright limestone scree on the floor of the hollow, the path continues up the gentle hillside across from the waterfall. Dwarf pines stand among limestone fragments, thicket, oleaster bushes.

It leads through beech woods and needle forests. Spruces, black pines. Occasionally a distant chiming from the valley – with any luck, a lengthy exchange, chiming in a winding series of slightly varied tonal sequences, a back-and-forth chiming, a for-and-against chiming, a zigzag chiming, the sources invisible, the direction indiscernible from the forest path.

Why this of all paths is the 'beautiful' one remains a mystery. Perhaps they call it that because it leads through a multitude of small landscapes, all manageable, each one spanning a few hundred, a few dozen steps: illustrations of the world. Fallen trees, felled by storms or tempests, boulders half-overgrown, the growth pattern of the trees above revealing the aisles they felled on their way down. Forests, meadows, small farm fields in clearings where garlic grows, unlocked shepherd's huts and cow pastures, boulders, swamps, rivers, brooks, arid terrain. Traces of water's abundance, traces of drought. Traces of mudslides, traces of flooding. An abundance of stone. Occasionally the view opens up to the mountains all around. Monte Musi to the south. Canin in the northeast. Again and again, Monte Canin; one's gaze searches for it everywhere, for orientation, to affirm one's own place in the world. The river – nothing but a brook according to its name – rushes louder than the water dares in summer. As if it were rushing below the Earth's surface, in some invisible Beyond, in order to lend the hungry scree field weight and significance.

Every bend, every crossroad has its marker: lines carved into boulders, crooked crosses, small stacked stone pyramids. Messages for the initiated, memory aids, memorials. Reminders not to forget. At the lowest point of the path, near the fire house, lies a small plain, a grazing meadow, where no livestock graze. The scattered shepherd's huts and cowsheds have been repaired and cleaned up, as if an old farm were going back into business. This is where the Sunday clothing swap once took place. Few people were able to afford festive garments in addition to their everyday clothes. But on Sundays, whoever was able would go finely dressed to the early service at the valley church, and on their way home, when they reached this point, would swap their garments with poorer people, who attended the later service. Or at least that's what they say, in the reports and stories about better times.

The path climbs steeply out of the pasture, the escarpment covered by scrubby blueberry bushes, moss and heather.

At the cemetery outside the village, the path again meets the road. The cemetery is small, lined by high columbarium walls. On the iron-barred gate is a latch, which every visitor is requested to close behind them when leaving the cemetery. The walls with *fornetti*, the chambers for bones or urns, frame the burial yard, and the grave markers on the ground appear small, small as urns, the soil spread thinly over the rock; space for coffins must be limited. As in the other villages, here a small pool of last names is repeated in various combinations and constellations – the people were born, widowed, married in every sequence of four or five names. If one waited until old age to photograph a woman, her face would be marked by bewilderment and absentmindedness, staring blankly at a skimpy bouquet of wildflowers or a black handbag. Changes in marital status are noted only for women. The photographs of men show no trace of bewilderment. An in-lawed, connected world of siblings and young go-getters boasting with chainsaws or cars, of old boors and careworn, hurt, bewildered elderly women. Younger women with yearning or pride in their eyes, and upswept hair. Taken from the blunt angle photographers reserved solely for female portraits, her head ascending into the image from the lower right corner, she gazes upwards, an air of submissiveness about her face. Travel agents, saleswomen were once photographed in this manner for promotional material. An upward gaze on the gravestone or memorial cross, a look that saw its way out, much like the eyes of the portrayed. Individual plastic flowers are stuck in the grave vases, while never-wilting floral arrangements adorn the cement of small grave plaques. Perhaps the buried are looking forward to autumn, when the chrysanthemums arrive, yellow, white and rusty red, pails of flowers, whose days may be numbered, but which nevertheless have a few weeks. The flowers of death, luminous in the mornings after the first frost.

In summer goldmoss and St. John's wort spring forth from crevices between the stones. Lizards scurry across the graves and straight over the faces on the plaques. An old woman polishes a gravestone bearing a photograph of an old woman who resembles the cleaner herself. She is depicted in a state of demented rapture, smiling at a bouquet of pale knapweed flowers. Occasionally the iron-barred gate screeches, a watering can rattles. Ta Lipa Pot, the beautiful way, leads to the dead: here one can become acquainted with them and learn their names and faces. And so from the start the villagers might appear silhouetted by a series of shadows, which stand behind them or hover over their heads or tremble in the back of their profiles in the vibrating spring air and emphatically announce to the new arrival: You are not from here.

FABLE
A fable of the region goes like this:

An animal finds a letter. Let's say this animal is a hen. The hen reads the letter, it's an invitation to a party. Seven animals are invited. The hen, the rooster, the duck, the swan, the oriole, the goldfinch and the – . The final name is missing from the page. Each time the hen runs into an animal, she looks at the letter and goes over the list again: the hen, the rooster, the duck, the swan...and so on. She stops at the neighbour's yard and picks up the rooster. They go on together. Down in the valley they meet a duck, then a swan. Come along! the hen waves. They make it out of the valley and reach the large river. They take a break in a forest, where the oriole sings. Come along! the hen cries, you too are invited. As if someone had called out his name, the goldfinch also appears. The six of them push on, and eventually reach the plain, tired, exhausted and in no state for a party, but still searching for the final name to complete the list, along with hen, rooster, duck, swan, oriole and goldfinch. On the horizon the evening light already shimmers over the sea, where it appears – the butterfly. The riddle is solved, their joy is great, night falls.

MEMORY

Monte Canin is a limestone massif. It forms a high plateau with individual peaks rising out of it. The massif draws the valley to a close, ruling over it in the east. The eye meets its highest peak from so many different angles; depending on one's perspective it appears to either turn toward the lower *abe* summits at its side, or away from them. *Bábe* are women, Canin is a tooth, a dogtooth, pointy and rough and a bit crooked; in winter the snow hangs thinly in the shallow, crooked fissures on the south side, and on the east side it lies blue into summer, in the shadow of the peak.

OLGA

What is memory? It comes and goes as it pleases. It disappears and intrudes, and we can't do anything about it. I see the wall, I remember the *carbon*. I remember the *carbon*, and my memory of the earthquake returns. Just like that, everything is connected and interwoven. I hear chickens and think of my childhood in Venezuela. Of the sweet fragrant tree in the yard and spots of sun on the floor. Everything has changed, but all this is still there. Memory is something that is being forever woven. All that we see and hear and think and smell, everything is like a thread in this woven cloth of memory. The cloth becomes longer and longer; in old age it is so long it would practically stretch the valley's length, all folded tightly in one's head. And the blood in one's veins courses over it, ceaselessly, and tiny threads come loose and wash up some place else, and so you forget. But it's still lying somewhere in your head. Yes, what is memory? We ourselves are memory.

—

The river rises from the Canin massif stone and flows a good dozen kilometres through the valley into the Fella, the white river, which soon thereafter flows into the Tagliamento, and so to the sea, to the sea. The river has only rock to call its origin, white Canin limestone. Along the way it winds around boulders of various stone, a landscape speaking the language of the past, of translations, of displacements.

ANSELMO

Memory is like a shadow. It follows you wherever you go. And if you had none, perhaps you would be left standing there, as awkward as without a shadow. Like the story about the man who sold his shadow. Whoever sells their shadow goes through the world not leaving a trace. And if a person can no longer remember anything, it's as if they have no trace of the world left inside them. My grandmother forgot everything in her old age, she recognized no one, she no longer recognized the village, save for a lane or two: to the cemetery and to the field, where she always went, as if searching for something. There must

45

have been something still there, even if she no longer knew it by name. Sometimes she would sing. To herself, but beautifully. Something was there that she could still remember. But it was only for her.

—

Canin is a karst mountain. In a state of constant flux, karst is testimony to stone's inferiority to the power of water. In its barrenness karst demands the water that relentlessly eats away at it, forgetting what it has eaten. The nicks and chasms and cavities the water leaves behind are its memoryless traces.

GIGI

There isn't a whole lot I remember. I don't spend much time thinking about the past. About what happened. Still, you need a memory. Who would you be, if you forgot everything? But memory can be cruel, it can hurt you. Then it's better to forget. But no one can forget on command. Remembering on command – now that's possible. To say to yourself: This is how it was, and you see it before your eyes again, just as it had been. Or something close to it. But then other memories pop up, unprompted, and get in the way. You have no control over the type of memory. Or forgetting. When you have nothing to do, all is memory. When you're working in the forest, it is possible to forget. Or when you're up in Alpine pastures. Then you can look and look, and you can forget, but whatever you see will somehow become memory again. We are all damned to memory. To what remains in memory and what is forgotten.

The river's edge, between rocks: oleasters, alders, black poplars, aspens. Fast-growing copses prepared for injustice, for floods and tremors. Greyish green and pale green, nourished on limestone and two-faced in the wind. Further up the slopes: beeches, hazelnut bushes. The darker green of fern fronds. Open meadows, sparse grass. Goat terrain. Knapweeds. Bugles, sage and mint. In spring, pale green primroses. Then the yellow spurge cymes, becoming later reddish, as if they rusted. Pincushions. Crane's bills. Dog daisies. Small-leafed thyme, yarrows, wild chervil, wild marjoram. Something vetch-like and yellow. Bell flowers. Wild orchids. Timber is felled everywhere. A hand is laid on the forest at all times.

SILVIA

I have a good memory, it is easy for me to retain things. Things I've seen on television, for example. I have a lot of memories. But they're not ordered. What I see on television occasionally mixes with whatever's going on at the time. Once – I remember as if it were yesterday – I was watching Sanremo, and my parents were arguing. My father slapped my mother, and she tried to slap him back. I was just a child. But I still remember the song, and to this day in my mind it's about my parents' argument. I'm not sure if other people manage to keep their memories in order. It's not the kind of thing one usually talks about. Sometimes it seems to me that memory is a heap of shards. You sweep and sweep and the shards continuously spill and slide down, and by the next stroke of the broom they suddenly lie somewhere else. And they grind against one another, and release dust. The dust is also part of the heap of shards, and it grows, just as memories do. Lying on the surface is what one remembers, and the small splinters and grains of dust are what one forgets and then remembers anew, once the broom has gone over it enough times and the pile of shards has found a new order. And there is always this crunching sound, the soft clinking of shards and fragments.

—

In the pale, shadowless light, when the sun's hidden behind a thin layer of clouds, seen from the perspective of the valley the bare limestone fields and the whitish rock scar running across the sparsely greened expanses can be read as a script. A distorted picture of a course of events on the mountainside tablet facing southeast, where tiny distant figures occasionally walk, moving across the script, as if ordered to trace with their footsteps this sign, recognizable only in a certain light.

TONI

I remember a lot of things, I just never know how to talk about them. I often think about my childhood. But I can't tell stories about it any more. My mind is full of images, but they race past too quickly for me to say anything about them. Or even describe them. What I say has nothing to do with the images in my head. Then it's as if the words were another language. If I tell you about a memory, it becomes something else entirely. Something that no longer belongs to me. Maybe because I realize that whoever's listening to me never sees exactly what I see. That bothers me, although I know it's normal. No one can picture what I see in my mind, since no one has seen

48

with my eyes the thing that's in my memory. At least that's how it is for me. And after I've told of it, the memory is no longer the same. And that's near good as forgotten.

—

Some of the deepest cavities on Earth are found in Monte Canin. Gorges, shafts, chasms, *abissi* where whatever finds its way in will never finds its way back out to the light. Shafts of forgetting. What constitutes a cavity? Is it the absence of stone, soil, light – or the presence of walls enclosing it? The darkness within or the light without? When does *can't remember* become *forgotten, after all*? In the early days of geology there was a science of abyssology. A theory of shafts, chasms, voids where forgotten things lie trapped, like tonsil stones. Things lost.

MARA

My mother gave birth to nine children. Three died, three went abroad and never returned. At first they wrote occasionally, or sent a photograph, but eventually even that stopped. My mother began forgetting early on. She forgot the soup on the stove and the goats in the shed and her basket on the field. But if one of us became sick, without a word she walked to a spot where some herb grew, to remedy the illness. And she always knew where to find her favourite flowers. Sometimes she sat outside on the bench and rocked back and forth, speaking with her children dead and disappeared. She was still able to remember their names, but not ours. Had she forgotten us? I'm not sure. Although I cared for her, I was no one to her – she called me and my remaining siblings by random names, never by our own. And later, when I had to lock

49

her in her room, she would hit and scratch me. But her children who had disappeared, who had left – they were still with her. What does it mean to remember, what does it mean to forget? It's a way of keeping order. When it hurts. And in life, generally. Our heads would explode if we never forgot. And so would our hearts.

—

The river carries things off, lays aside and erodes things, washes away this and takes along that, seeps down, murmurs, plunges and exhales illusory lakes. It wants to go here and there, always distracting one from the shortness of its course, always questioning erratic rocks about their origins, alien to limestone. A landscape caught up in constant pulling and abrading and wiping away traces, in revealing the unreliable witness that is terrain. On tranquil days the shadows of birds flying across the river fall down to the rocky ground, and yet leave behind nothing on the river. No darkness, no movement to bring them across the water.

LINA
I like talking about the past. About my memories. With my siblings, my friends. When acquaintances who left the valley a long time ago visit, we all sit around talking. Time and again things are rescued from oblivion. Occasionally we disagree about something; everyone wants to be right. I believe I'm able to remember many things precisely. I like thinking about the past. I go through the list of my schoolmates' names. Who sat in which seat. When did this or that happen. What was the weather like. Calamities and strokes of luck. My own, other people's. Sometimes I

write down a memory, but it's nothing like talking about your memories. I write them down in a small notebook. My notebook lies hidden in a drawer; I don't think anyone has found it and taken a look yet. I know what to expect if someone does: But that's not how it was at all! Yeah, then you tell me how it was, I would reply, you tell me! How was it? And then we would go back and forth, and the beautiful memory would lie in a thousand pieces.

—

Does the mountain have a memory? Do the footsteps survive somewhere? What about the sounds? Hand movements? Groping, gripping, sliding, digging. The shuffling, rubbing, searching footfalls? The hoofbeats of animals, the grazing of wings, the sharpening of a beak against stone. The bird calls, the intermittent human voices – perhaps it is a pattern, furrowed into surfaces by the tones, these tiny veined furrows scratched out by sounds, by the forever returning, echoing bird calls; effected by the whistling wind, by the tiny fall of loose particles that follows this or that call, these networked grooves that the air brushes over, making it buzz – incessant, ascending in thin waves: the plummeting, inaudible, dauntless sound of memory.

TRIBUTARIES
The *torrente* – as the word suggests, more of an impetuous brook than a river – has many tributaries. From every fissure and gorge and every mountain trench, water flows, in accordance with its name either black or white or dry or cold or cloudy or murky or quick, named after mountain pastures, after hunters, after animals, after

legendary figures, borders, trees, the position of the sun. Here every piece of earth and every arm's length of water has a name, and along with its name comes a story, or the story behind a story. The water dictates the terrain and determines the paths, carries some things off and brings around others, leaving behind recesses, crevasses, fissures, gorges in the soft stone made of discarded shells, husks, fish bones, spines, lives – the *abissi* that limestone explorers pressed their ears against, listening out for the most distant echo of a sign of life.

ABYSS

An old path leads to a high mountain meadow with *stavoli*: huts on the alpine pastures where in former times summer lives were lived. It leads from the valley road across the river, passing by the Massa dei Morti, the rock of the dead, on the bridge. Casket bearers coming from more distant villages, carrying a corpse to what was then the valley's only cemetery, would take a break here at this boulder and put down the coffin. The entire funeral procession would stop and the bereaved would serve the casket bearers a refreshment they had brought along. Wine, cheese, bread.

Every burial was an event, especially if harsh weather had made digging a grave impossible. Whoever could spare the hours joined the funeral procession. If a man was to be buried, the men came along; if it was a woman, the women came along, at times bringing their children. The cortèges of men were silent or accompanied by a cloud of murmuring; the women's cortèges were louder from song. They sang not only sad songs, but also songs about the landscape or love. It depended on the dead, on how they had died.

52

Long after the villages in the valley all had their own cemeteries, people still stopped here, in order to place their hands on the rock beside the path, or even to kiss this stone, in remembrance of the funeral procession intermissions. Later an altar was erected against forgetting, a small theatre box with the Madonna – a protagonist paralyzed by mild sadness.

The path ascends steeply behind the old cemetery across the river, passing through a beech forest, then a ravine, the earthy slopes entirely traversed by roots, and growing in the shadows and north-facing terrain are winter roses, a shade-loving plant said to drive out one insanity with another. Once out of the ravine, there is a sweeping view across the valley and up to the hillsides rising to Canin. From here it is clear that Canin is not a mountain but a massif, a ridge with several peaks with depressions and declivities between them, and one recognizes that the continuation of this massif, the two *bábe*, are larger than one is led to believe from further away, and that there is a third, smaller *bába*, entirely hidden from other angles, nothing more than a small hillock, perhaps a third little sister the legend forgot.

For centuries, the valley municipalities fought over Canin (but which massif peak?) and none involved were satisfied until eventually the peak, the highest point and the obvious curvature below it, the slopes and the saddle, were all awarded to the municipality farthest from the mountain, at the end of the valley, practically on Statale 13, as if to release the other, smaller villages from their argument by uniting them in their rage against that one, distant place that had its back turned to them and couldn't even see the mountain.

The slope climbs to a large forest of black pines, sitting above on the ridge, solemn and dark. Behind a bend the path once again enters the forest, mottled by sunlight, violets growing on the waysides in spring, wrinkled primrose leaves and grey-veined heart-shaped cyclamen foliage. Waiting beyond the forest path is a view onto a smaller, gorge-like valley with broad, cleared areas on gentler slopes above the gorge gap. For short stretches the path proceeds across bare rock, close to the abyss; in one location a spur of rock has broken off sharply. From the other side of the valley the precipitous breaking point appears yellowish, a vague smudged orange-reddish colour. At the height of the rock spur breakage, on the wayside – and, it should be said, dizzyingly near to the edge of the abyss – is a wooden plaque. It shows a man in an animal-skin cloak surrounded by goats. It's the kind of depiction typical of a picture book about the world of the mountains: shepherd, goats, a panorama of snow-covered peaks surrounded by green mountain pastures – nothing like the actual view from this location. The picture is already somewhat faded from time and the elements, and coated in a fine network of small fissures. Craquelure. If it weren't for the missing horns, the man in a goat's hide could be taken for a goat himself, walking upright, or at least an animal, that's how closely his cloak resembles fur, how small the outline of his head, seen only from behind. The man on the plaque is named Gigi. He allegedly disappeared here, along with his small herd. He wandered the country alone and was a recluse, as they say, and he disappeared, or rather his disappearance was noted, when they discovered this rockslide, caused by an imperceptible tremor, and several stories continue making rounds in the valley about Gigi's end and his goats, said to have all jumped in after him. But no one was there to bear witness, and recluses who avoid people can be gone a long time before anyone notices their absence; it is a saga creeping

54

down this rock spur. The boulder is visible, lying deep in the gorge, yet it cannot be accessed from any side, and even with the most powerful binoculars it would not be possible to glimpse the remains of some creature buried below the boulder, be it human or animal, creatures that moved through time and space until they met their end here. Bones, fur, things not stone. It is a commemorative plaque that stands here, and on it one might see a certain mythical creature. And at the same time, it is a path marker. Gigi's *abisso*. It leads to the mountain pastures if you keep to the path after it turns away from the abyss.

II

'Whereas the subterranean roar is understood to be a nearly constant, and one almost wants to say necessary, companion to the earthquake, many of the other frequently cited accompanying phenomena are in contrast merely coincidentally simultaneous events, although one is inclined to see them, too, in a causal relationship with the earthquake. This includes e.g. peculiar fog, heavy gusts of wind, thunderstorms and other electrical phenomena, emissions of steam and gasses, etc....

As far as earthquake *omens* first and foremost are concerned, one can arguably conclude that, aside from the weaker tremblings of the ground that often precede more severe shocks, and aside from the occasional preluding roar, we can presume no further definite and unfailing heralds of these terrible and destructive events.... For what one wants to regard as such an omen, whether it is about the character of the weather or status of the barometer or the appearance of fiery meteors or the behaviour of animals and the state of the people – how often these things do take place, *without* being followed by an earthquake!'
—— Carl Friedrich Naumann, *Essentials of Geology*, vol. 1 (1850)

LANDSCAPE

From a height, from the karstic domes below the peak of Monte Canin the entire valley is visible, expanding irregularly in gentle rises and small, stage-like plateaus encircled by mountains. The villages are on higher ground, some protected by cliffs. Those with a more attractive position, surrounded by open country, fell victim to the earthquake almost entirely. Ruins here, overly meticulous lines of white town houses there, angular interlopers in a region smoothed by wind and water and stone against stone. Outside the housing developments are disinterred stones, moraines, collected material resistance to the movement. Meadows, pastures, small strips of cultivated land. Higher up, separated from the villages by steep, forested slopes are alpine pastures and high meadows. Abundant stone. The rivers, brooks, rivulets write themselves into the valley, white marks and lines of doggedness, where furrowing into solid ground is the only goal. The paths, the roads all write in a different, clumsier script of negotiated accessibility. Where from, where to. No way out of the valley in sight, mountains all around; from the blue-forested hillsides and jagged angular rock faces to the grey and purple furrows and chutes and the toothy peak and yellowish fractures and wounded mountain surfaces: in every direction the horizon is lost.

ANSELMO

At first we wanted to go out, my sister and I, out at any cost, once everything began to sway; Don't go out! our father bellowed, yanking us below the doorframe, his hands like iron. Plaster and mortar crumbled down, a piece of wall caved in, we couldn't see anything or breathe from the dust, and I had to think of the gravel pit in Germany, where my sister and I hid in a cave when asked to choose between staying with our mother and returning to Italy with our father. In the cave sand crumbled down onto us in the same way, all of a sudden, and we couldn't breathe and were afraid. I'll never forget it, we both wet our pants. I can't remember how long the earthquake lasted, an hour or a minute. Outside people were screaming. We couldn't use the front door and had to cross the yard. Stones and soil everywhere. In my memory it was still light outside, but it couldn't possibly have been light outside. A neighbour lay in the road, perhaps knocked down by fear, or something had hit her; she groaned as my father and a neighbour picked her up – they wanted to carry her, but then they didn't know where. A large crack ran down our street. I think the sky was green, dark green. I was cold. Then I remembered I'd been playing at the window with my Indian, the only piece of my wild west fort that I had brought along when we returned to Italy with my father. The fort stays here, my mother said at the time, as we packed, and that was worse than anything. But I had the Indian in my trouser pocket, she didn't know that. The Indian was the first thing I thought of. I stood on the street beneath a green sky, thinking about the Indian and wondering if it was still by the window. I can't remember going back into the house to look for it, or when it was that I did – maybe the next day. Everything was full of dust and plaster fragments, and the windowsill was crooked. I found the Indian right away. And I was also able to rescue my fiddle, but already that evening, directly after the earthquake or while it was still happening; the instrument survived nearly unscathed, aside from the coarse dust inside it, and a scratch. You never know what will occur to you in an emergency, and then everything warps. Until then the Indian had always reminded me of

Germany – it was my German Indian – but after 6 May it became my Earthquake Indian. Whenever I saw it, I thought of the earthquake. And how I couldn't breathe from the dust.

VIPERS

The viper is a native poisonous snake. It shelters in the many hollows and cracks in the rock and in winter can retreat into the stone and earth shot through with hollows; tunnellers and road workers frequently report finding knots of entwined vipers while breaking through masses of rock.

The viper is well adapted to its surroundings and among rocks and stone and on the soil it is difficult to spot. It seldom attacks, shies from noise and often goes stiff as a stick when humans approach. But whoever walks inattentively, falls, stumbles, reaches their hand into a sparse bush on stony ground will startle it. You can recognize a viper by its triangular, flat head. Catching a viper is a test of courage, but after extensive practice it can become a desirable skill one can earn money with. You have to be swifter than the small animal, lightning quick and spirited of hand as you reach out to grab it, taking care that your thumb presses the base of its neck and the animal no longer can move its head. The helpless body continues to resist by whipping itself around with great force, but if your grip on its head is tight and the tip of your thumb remains rigid and unfaltering on the thin bones at the base of its skull, the body is ineffective. The captured snakes are let into bottles and brought to the pharmacist, who purchases them at a small price. The pharmacist extracts poison from the snake's tooth, for medicinal purposes. Live vipers fetch a better price than dead ones.

MARA

The earthquake was an event in my life that I'll never forget. Maybe it's the only thing that will remain in my memory always, until the hour of my death. What comes next, no one knows. Do you remember things even after you've died? I was anxious that entire evening. The late afternoon light was so piercing and nevertheless opaque, as if you could reach out and grab it, all viscous. I broke into a sweat cleaning up, and my top stuck to my back – I was only wearing my chemise – and then, while I was cleaning up, that's when it began. First this wind howling in the yard all of a sudden, and then something fell down outside and I began to freeze, abruptly. Then this sound. This dark rolling. It was so alive. At first I thought it was the dog growling; all day she had acted so deranged, I might have thrown a rock at her head – and I had even given her the rest of my soup after I finished eating. Anyway, the growling began, at first very far away – or, no, not far away, but from way deep down – I'd just finished cleaning up when the ground began to tremble under my feet, and a can fell from the shelf, bouncing, and the entire kitchen smelled of yarrow; the key, the key, I shouted – to myself because my mother was still in her room, and now she was utterly silent. In my apron, I remembered, snatching the key from the pocket, and rushing to her room, where the walls were already cracking, yet aside from the growling and the groaning inside the walls, it was so quiet; I pulled my mother from the daybed where she sat and brought her outside, she had loosened her braid and her hair was already full of white grit, and she took very small steps, like a child who wants to appear dainty, like a princess, and all the while it seemed to me that everything around us would collapse at any moment, that's the kind of noise, yet it was a dull sound; maybe nothing at all had fallen

61

there yet, and that came later, but I left the yard for the path and briefly thought: now it looks as if I were leading mother to the altar, and to top it off she had these white speckles in her hair. But no one noticed us, there was a bang and people screamed, and the dogs barked, and I noticed I was in my chemise, and my mother had peed herself again – I hadn't smelled it until then, but what could I have done, anyway, if I had smelled it earlier? And so we stood there like an order no one picked up, as they say, although I don't think that occurred to me at the time. I say it now, after so many years, but that bit about the bride has always been with me; it's more like an image, always the same, all terror and broken things and the bride on my arm.

An earthquake rattles everything and turns it upside down, even the thoughts in your head. I can't remember what I did with my mother. Did I sit her down outside? We lived on the slope, and a narrow stairway led past the other houses up to the road. We had always looked onto the patched roof of our neighbour below us. He had put down various layers of tar paper and corrugated sheet iron, one on top of the other, nothing but these patchwork pieces he had somehow managed to get his hands on. Beneath this was his shed. The roof had caved in, the shed below it too, and the patched-up roof pieces protruded every which way. I stood there, feeling as if I could hear the river below, the rushing of the water, as always. Had the elderflower bloomed, on the slope leading down to the river? The gaunt lilac bush in front of our house? And where did I seat my mother? I must have put on a dress, after all. I don't know any more.

Our house was barely damaged – a miracle, I thought, again and again. A few windows broken. That crack in the rear wall, but it wasn't so bad. Just dust everywhere, fragments of plaster, mortar, scattered limestone dust, patches of limestone fallen from the ceiling.

We must have walked down to the road after all, because I remember talking to other people about where to spend the night. We were all afraid to go back into our houses. But I didn't know where else to go, and in the end I took my mother home. I can still remember how our neighbour below was already yanking equipment out of his broken shed. Inside the house I shook out my mother's bedsheets. I didn't wash her, although she had soiled herself. Maybe I just took off her pants and laid her back in bed, in her room. But I didn't lock the door. She whimpered quietly. I'm right here, mother, I called out to her. I lay down in the backyard on the bench below the awning. I heard animals screaming in the village – barns had collapsed as well, the animals were frightened. The lowing of a cow – I'll never get it out of my head. This quake rolled in below us again and again, and every time I thought: This thing is alive. After every quake something fluttered or crumbled again somewhere. It turned cold, and it rained. Sleep never came. Or maybe just a little. I wasn't afraid, but I had this feeling, very foreign to me, foreign and immense, as if it were the end of days. The chickens in their coop – not once did I check on them, the building stood solid as ever. Were the chickens screeching? I can't remember. My thoughts circled, that I remember very well. Everything that occurred to me – the eggs in the basket, the herbs in the airing cupboard, the socks I had started knitting, the vegetable patch. How would my brother make it home on his knife grinder's bicycle? And what if he never came back? Whenever my mother whimpered I called out: I'm right here, mother. I think my mother is the only one who slept inside just as every other night. Nothing happened to us.

CUCKOO

The cuckoo arrives in early April and its call rings throughout the entire valley. The hens, with their jigging, polysyllabic call, prefer to remain in the bosk along the river, scouting out nests to lay their eggs in. The males, with their two-note call, are found closer to the gardens. The host birds become wiser each year and occasionally try to drive out the cuckoo hen from the valley. But never are they successful more than once. The cuckoo hen is an excellent scout, and swift. She requires mere seconds to lay her egg, and then she flies off with the nest egg in her beak. Once hatched, the cuckoo young gape their beaks so wide that the host parents become afraid and panic. These delicate foster parents exhaust themselves, stuffing the maws they themselves would fit inside. On the day of the earthquake only the males called out, all day long. The females remained silent. By its former name the cuckoo was known as gowk – the fool, as in jester: it was the manor fool, the whooping jester, before it was confined to its own call.

OLGA

The day of the earthquake was extremely hot, but that evening a sudden wind came; I stood in the kitchen drying dishes while my aunt sat by the radio, and all of a sudden an icy gust burst in, causing the window to slam against the cabinet. And then a thundering of sorts rose from the earth, running beneath our feet, and then the first blow. My aunt screamed, and my father – he was there, too – and he shoved us out of the kitchen. We all wanted to go out into the open but my father held onto us, and we stayed in the threshold of the hall, where the walls were thickest, that was the oldest part of the house.

Window panes shattered and plaster broke off the walls, pictures fell to the floor, and everything rattled, the entire house groaned. Outside we heard screams and children crying; maybe everything was briefer and happened faster than I'm telling it now, but that's how it always is in memory and when speaking of things past. Words take longer than the thing or event itself. It is no different with a dream. Recounting a dream takes forever, and in the end the dream is no longer what it had been. My cousins were in Germany at the time, working construction. That was for the best, since it meant two fewer heads without a roof. Where should we have gone? We didn't have a car. We had a difficult time getting out. The vestibule had collapsed, my father had just built it that autumn. There were chunks of masonry behind us, too, and plaster fluttered from the ceiling, from between the exposed beams. The air was full of dust, and I'd scraped my hand. We exited on the side, through the kitchen, and the shed where we kept our firewood stood crooked, all the firewood fallen down, and we had to climb over it to get to the road. The neighbours across from us had an outdoor kitchen that collapsed, and I could hear people screaming inside, or from under the collapsed wall – I can't remember any more – and my father immediately jumped in to help, and I wanted to go with my aunt to the square – because where else should we have gone? I saw women carrying children down the lane, and it rumbled, and I think the sky thundered as well, and occasionally everything became so silent, so silent, but maybe that's just something I imagine today. That evening I found a small cat, pressing itself against a wall.

During the earthquake part of the ceiling gave way, upstairs. In a few places you could see the roof timbering through the cracks and holes. Everything was covered in a white dust. Our beds, our clothing – everything. And the doors and windows hung askew in the hinges. Every day there were aftershocks, and every time, the fear came, regardless of where you stood. Although from day to day you got used to it. Our fear shrank. Or it became familiar.

Back then the worst thing was sleep. Whoever had a car let their children sleep inside, while the adults remained outside, if possible in shelters built from sticks and fabric, until the soldiers came and brought us tents. But it was difficult to sleep. We were afraid to sleep, afraid of the dark, afraid the droning and quaking might hit us unprepared, although that just as well happened in the bright light of day. From my shelter I saw the wooden veranda, hanging completely askew. A few days later it became detached even further. Later my cousins tore it down and built a balcony of stone. Today no one remembers how the house looked before the stone balcony. I can only remember the crooked veranda, the way it hung there, entirely ripped out from the wall, only holes where the beams had been anchored in the masonry. At the sight of the veranda I think it hit me that nothing would ever be the same again. I sensed it. And at the time we didn't even know what had happened in other places. I was saving up for a Vespa.

GOATSUCKER

The nightjar is a crepuscular and nocturnal bird. It spends its days motionless on the ground, or in branches. Its feathers are a grey brown, flecked and striped by rusty and dark tones: thus camouflaged, the motionless bird blends in with its surroundings and does not attract attention. Barely perceptible on the stony, earthy ground among thin blades of grass and brush. The eyes alone glimmer, but this is recognizable only from very close up. The nightjar does not build a nest, instead laying its eggs directly on the naked ground. But even without building a nest, it still always seeks the same location. It reaches the valley in April and fills the evening twilight and the darkness with its gurgling purrs, a rising and falling, a vibrating tone that can be heard from far away, causing the entire countryside to undulate, soft and wavering minutely in its pitch, just like the music of the region. The nightjar has arrived, the people say, it is spring. *Succiacapre*. The goatsucker. How did it get this name? Perhaps its gurgling and trilling begins when the goats are milked for the first time after winter.

GIGI

On that day back then, we were felling down in the valley; I still remember it clearly, because that evening I went to the village by way of the cemetery. It was so hot, that wasn't normal. We mentioned it only in passing, but it was unusual. Now it seems to me that was also the day we saw two fawns. Totally alone. They stood still at a distance while we unpacked our equipment. Without fear. Like two children, who just wanted to watch. I motioned to the others to keep quiet. I didn't want them to startle the fawns. But then suddenly they were gone. Entirely silent, inaudible. We didn't hear a sound. Not a branch snapping. As if they had flown off.

We don't talk much while we work. Only the most necessary commands. We always take turns or alternate the tasks, depending on the number of people and height of the tree. One person directs, to make sure the tree falls in the right direction. At lunchtime I went home, it wasn't too far away. The large white stone field beneath the snow on the mountain looked so yellow. I still remember that. There had been a rockslide there, years ago, in a gully. Since then this white field has been there. A man from the village allegedly went missing for good in that rockslide. And the people said this white patch looked like a person, standing there with open arms. If you looked at it closely, you could see it. Maybe the missing person just up and left. For the valley and beyond. Gone. Or he fell into one of the rock crevices. They are so deep, no human knows how many metres.

The shed was heavily damaged in the earthquake. The goats found a safe place to stand. Goats are intelligent animals. They trembled like the ground, yet they were in one piece. Who knows at what point they had felt the disaster coming, whereas we noticed nothing until the rumbling, once it was already too late. All hell had been let loose. The neighbour across the way with the boxy house smacked his children, who had run out before he said to; who knows, maybe he wanted the house to fall on their heads. His mother hopped out the window, a couple of hard-willed demons they were, the old woman and he, and these two stubborn German children. Outside in the lanes people were screaming, and the dogs, the dogs – that had been going on all evening, but now their barking mingled with all the screams. My mother ran out of the house. Where is your father! Where is your father! she called out. Where else would he be? He was at the tavern. My mother stood in her slippers, the crucifix beneath her arm, and the picture of my grandparents, the large framed one. Her new Virgin Mother, which glowed in the dark, was in her apron pocket, shimmering blue-green through the fabric of her apron. The Virgin Mother could also be made to flicker, like a blinking light. It was for the window, my mother had explained to me, so everyone would see it. Our house appeared fully intact, the damages emerged only later. At first you didn't see a thing, or at least not from outside. I felt the breath of the goats, all warm and quick and wet.

The wind came in gusts, as if thrust by the quake, and then the chimney toppled, as though blown off, and directly beside my mother a brick crashed to the ground; I grabbed her arm and led her to the street, then returned to the goats. A cold rain set in, and along with it, the wind, this screaming, the animals bellowing in their sheds. From the house came the scent of thick smoke; the chimney had collapsed inward. Outside I found a bucket of mop water; I took it inside and dumped it on the stove. Everything was covered in shards; a panel was torn out of the door, I returned to the goats and then brought them up into the forest.

STONE

Karstic limestone is a rock formed of living organisms: an accumulation of life lived and life's traces, grown into a dense mass that in turn becomes the backdrop and the substrate of life. The karstic mass is susceptible to weathering. Susceptible to the accumulation of traces and their erasure. A stone in flux that can be relied on for little, with a tendency to form caves and abysses, which takes pleasure in falling and is well-established among avalanches. Like a monster in a fairy tale, the limestone mountain always needs a victim. The gravelly mass provides for its own vivification, yielding grasses, spawning seeds, letting itself be colonized, creating its own world.

TONI

In the nights after the earthquake, we children slept in the car – all five of us in one Fiat. From the window I saw the tip of the church steeple. Because ours was still standing.

The adults walked around outside, searching and clearing. Searching – I think that was the main thing at first. Searching for people, searching for animals, searching for things. Everyone searched for something. Were there animals trapped somewhere? They listened for signs of life in the piles of wooden beams and collapsed walls. In our area only two or three people had been trapped – they were freed – but in other villages in the valley it was more, and some people even lost their lives. We heard about it later. An entire village was destroyed. For days they called and searched for animals. There were also things to secure. Money and identification papers and valuables. Watches. But where to put them? Everything was in chaos. Everyone was constantly trying to repair something. To tidy up. Whenever someone entered a house someone else had to accompany them, in order to stand watch outside, lest something collapse inside and injure whoever had gone in. It was so cramped in the car; the windows were cracked, and raindrops fell inside. And the animals. We had to care for the animals. In the night of the earthquake the village cows lowed as if their sheds were ablaze. And the dogs barked and howled. They'd already been doing that all day; everyone had noticed, but no one anticipated its meaning. Afterwards you're always wiser. Since then I get an eerie feeling whenever I hear dogs howling and barking for reasons I do not know. There are nights like that, always have been, when one dog's agitation infects the others – all it takes is a sound, footsteps, an animal, and one dog gets started, and before long all the village dogs join in, one by one. Dujak, the old people always say, it's Dujak walking through the village – Dujak left the forest and has plans in the village, so whatever you do, stay inside, or Dujacesa will bring you back to the forest. Dujak is the savage. His partner is Dujacesa. They live in the forest. That's what we say in our language that only we understand. A form of Russian, our teacher once said – but Russians don't understand us, either. He had been in Moscow and showed us pictures and read us a few sentences from a book. Moscow is an enormous city with districts larger than this entire valley, full of high-rise buildings. Twenty, thirty stories high. An earthquake would be worse there than here. I lay in the car, trying to picture it, wondering if the high-rises would sway and tip over or if they would collapse, as a few houses had here. Not many. Almost all the house walls were left standing. You can walk through Moscow for years without ever crossing anyone's path, my teacher told us back then. But who walks for years, aside from in fairy tales? Not even our teacher.

BURNING BUSH

In May the verges of deciduous forests are abloom with burning bush. The flower has migrated here from the stony hillsides of Crete, they say; in summer the seed capsules burst open, flinging their seeds metres away. The flower thus migrates from one chalky soil to the next, crossing seas in wanderers' pockets and in the folds of their clothing, settling where it can; once in a while the sun shines down so hotly on it that the lemon-scented gas emanated by the flowers ignites into small, silent blue flames which nevertheless harm neither the plant nor the pink-veined flowers.

SILVIA

I had just arrived home with my father. He let me sit on the back of his moped while he pushed. We didn't have far to go. He leaned the moped against the shed, and I went inside. My father always washed himself first, in the laundry room out in the yard. I think it suddenly became very cold outside. I felt a bit strange from sitting on the moped, my legs like rubber, and as I went into the house the ground beneath me moved; I thought it was because of the moped. My grandmother grabbed hold of me and shoved me outside into the yard, where tiles had already fallen from the roof, and I screamed and wanted to go back into the house but my grandmother held onto me tight, pushing me in front of her; outside the people were already screaming and everywhere there was a bang, and clouds of dust rose in the air, and I saw our shed fall down, as if it were made of paper; in my memory it all happened very slowly, my grandmother pushing me ahead, the shed falling, and then I saw the moped, the part of it sticking out from under pieces of the shed. I thought my father had died. But then suddenly he was there, and we three stood in the street. What happened afterwards is all a jumble for me, the noise and the screaming, and everyone so afraid. And I was so cold, I'll never forget it, never since have I been so cold. My leg was bleeding, and so was my arm, but I can't remember how I hurt myself. Later my father brought me to an acquaintance of his, so I could sleep in a car with other children. It was very cramped and that was terrible, and the windows always fogged; it rained outside and the other children didn't want me to crack the window, but I did anyway and the boy beside me whacked me in the back and said he would kick me out, but I couldn't stand not being able to look out the window. He didn't kick me out but instead kneed me all night long, on purpose I think. A long, wide crack ran down the street – that I remember – but I don't think I saw it until the next day. Whoever had a car had it good, because that was a shelter, of sorts. Driving away was not a possibility: the roads were all full of stones and rooftiles and pieces of houses. The next day my father fashioned a makeshift tent, but inside it was cold. A part of our house's roof had collapsed, everything downstairs was in disarray. It was dirty, but nothing looked destroyed. On her last visit my mother had brought me a pair of shoes, black patent leather shoes that buckled, and at first I couldn't find them, since they were entirely white from the dust. I wanted to go call my mother but my father yelled at me, Why should I worry about your mother, she is sitting in safety. The telephone at the bar didn't work yet. Telephone and electricity lines were down, and it would be days before the power was back on. The Alpini had already arrived by then, bringing my mother along with them. She sat in the back of a wagon, among all the soldiers in her thin dress. Maybe she had forgotten how cold it was around us.

DEVIL'S CLAW
Devil's claw is a flower of barrenness that grows out of limestone, out of the cracks and fissures where a layer of earth has settled. The leaves are dark green, shiny and toothed. From the centre of a wreath of leaves projects the stem, with a dome of many onion-shaped blooms ending in a pointy spur, twirled and often forked. The blooms are light purple, almost white at the outermost curves, whereas the tips of the blooms and the spurs are dark purple. The flower often grows horizontally out of the rock crevices and, among the grey and pale green of the rocks

and scanty grasses, appears like an animate being that has decided to lean out into the world.

LINA

On the evening of the earthquake I heard Milena next door, laughing her crazy, rough, shrill laugh that had already pursued me for days. A few years earlier she became sick in her head, her husband said. Really sick, with a high fever and inflammation of the brain. After that, Milena had these attacks. She would let out this loud, shrill, cutting laugh which was no joke. Occasionally she would yell: Get out! Or: May I come in? May I come in? I can still hear it. They kept the blinds closed, I only saw her when she was in the yard. She talked to her dahlias. But her dahlias – they were gorgeous, in every colour, no one had dahlias as beautiful as she. Her husband wasn't from around here. Everyone just called him the *veneziano*, because that's where he was from, from the Veneto. Down below. Not many people came to the valley and stayed. That was an act of love. He could sing so beautifully, songs unlike those we sing here, he sang pop songs more than anything else, sometimes opera. Apparently it calmed Milena. That's what he said, anyway. He would sing 'La mia valle', which I always liked to hear, although in his case it was the other way around, since *he* came to her in the valley. Music like that calmed her the most. He would sing to her for hours, and she just whimpered on occasion, and by the end was entirely silent. In any case, she had been having these attacks for days. In this way insane people are a bit like animals, or so they say. They have a different instinct. They can feel it when something dark approaches. However that may be, after the earthquake she was utterly silent. Not a sound.

At our place things broke during the earthquake in various ways. A bedroom collapsed, our dishes fell from the shelf in the kitchen, between the house door and the yard a rift opened up. The earth gaped. One of my brothers was drunk, we had to pull him into the house and he constantly bent over for things on the ground. Once outside, I headed over to Milena and her husband to help them. Both were entirely mute from fear. Milena had a small laceration on her head, nothing too bad. Maybe something had fallen on her head, or in her fright she bumped into something. Their house was less damaged than ours, only a large mirror lay in a thousand shards. That's bad luck, they both said, simultaneously, as if speaking from a single mouth, they really howled. But we've already got bad luck, I answered, I don't know why I was so calm.

I led them to the small square in front of the bar, where a few people had already gathered, the elderly above all. Someone had brought along a powerful flashlight, like a search light. The electricity was out. Then I went back.

It is impossible to describe the pervading state of excitement and fear. The animals cried. I entered the chicken coop, which was still standing, feeling my way in with my hands, it smelled pungent, more pungent than usual, like the shit of so many chickens. The chickens all stood crowded into a corner, at least that's how I remember it, and it's as if I had seen them, but after all it was dark. Thankfully we didn't have any cows or pigs back then. What do you do with a pig, in its hovel below the kitchen, it too in the end buried alive below the rubble? Later people often said they would have saved their pig quicker than their own wife. The dogs howled and barked on all sides. I felt utterly helpless. In my mind thoughts raced, about things and people, little things that I wanted to save occurred to me, my notebook with jottings, I think I even

75

went once more back into the house in the dark. I can't remember. Somehow an image has stayed with me, of the village as seen from my window, the dots of the flashlights in the dark, the shadows on the road, the calls, the screams, out of the dark, the scratching and ripping and trickling and hoisting wherever they thought someone might lie buried. What is truth, what is imagination when it comes to an experience like this? It's as if branded in my memory, but it's also different when you remember or talk about it. The next day someone carried his broken fiddle around the village, as if it were his child.

The first time I entered our house again in daylight I saw the stones and chunks of mortar on my bed. In the dusky light one could have mistaken it for the outline of a person asleep. As if *I* lay there, from stone, turned to stone. I don't remember what I thought at that moment, whether I was frightened, whether I calmed myself down – I don't know. Only that the sight of it has never left me.

THISTLE
The thistles are native to the valley. Composite plants, whose blooms conform to a sphere, to the inflorescences of a second order. The steel-blue blossoms begin sprouting at the top of the spherical head and proceed downward. In autumn the spherical heads are carried off by the wind, rolling across the ground and dispersing their seeds, which thrive even between stones. Despite its thorns, the thistle is believed to be friendly and curative: a keeper of order in the barren land.

OLGA

It doesn't matter where I am: whenever I hear the swift singing in the evening, I think about the earthquake. Or I think about life back then in the valley, and then I think about the earthquake. Swifts always call out in the evening, in summer; they migrated early, but as long as they were there, in the evening they set the tone in the village. You can never be sure if their call is anxious or glad – these sharp tones, this screeching – and how they chase one another, forever circling. I remember the screaming birds on the evening before the earthquake, or perhaps I only think I remember it; at times I also remember a vast silence. How did the birds fare, in expectation of the earthquake? Of all animals, birds must have been least afraid, since nothing can happen to them up there in the heavens, and they don't even sense the ground. And what do we even know about the language of birds? As soon as we put it in our own words, whatever the bird said is lost. Fear! Do birds know fear? Chickens, perhaps. In Venezuela our chickens were afraid every time my grandmother entered the yard; she held the butcher's knife behind her back, and yet still they were afraid – they always knew when she came to kill. But I would like to know how it appeared to the birds when boulders rolled and houses collapsed and then of course this dull droning, it must have given every creature a scare. I once watched a solar eclipse. The light changed at first slowly, then very quickly, and the birds chirruped with increasing nervousness. It was midday, and suddenly the shadows grew rapidly, more shadows than darkness. Once the light had altogether disappeared, the birds fell utterly silent. It was a hush unlike anything I'd ever heard. Not like in the night, since nocturnal animals make noises, after all. But the animals and birds of the night hardly had time to wake up. And just like that, the entire world fell silent. A few minutes later the light came back by degrees, and the birds began singing as they do in the early morning. Just a bit quicker, or at least that's how it seemed to me. After all, it grew light quicker than it does in the morning.

In the days after the earthquake it rained and even snowed, so the swifts didn't fly their evening circles. They remained in their nests, and occasionally one heard them chirping.

Sometimes I wake up in the night feeling as if my mouth were full of dust. The taste of mortar dust and chalk. Now I will suffocate, I think, now I am buried below the rubble and will suffocate. In my nose and in my mouth I still have this memory, as if it were embossed, and I can never be sure when it will awaken. However that may be, something wakes it, sometimes while I'm sleeping, sometimes abruptly in the middle of the day, at work, while I'm watching television. But it always passes, and I don't suffocate.

ORCHIS MACULATA

The moorland spotted orchid is a flower with a design flaw, blooming on low-moor bogs and in open dry forests after the first cuckoo chicks have hatched. The lip bears the spur backwards and opens up, pale purple to white, to bumblebees, who lose their way in the nectarless calyxes. Like small herds, the cuckoo flowers stand together in groups and at twilight emit a pallid light, like autumn crocuses. Here they are known as *concordia* due to the concord of their tubers, of which only one – and only the flower knows which – is able to reproduce.

ANSELMO

We drove out of Germany in the evening. A friend of my father picked us up in a car, my father, my sister and me and our suitcases. It was winter. My mother stood at the open door, it was already growing dark, light burned inside, she didn't even wave. We took the night train, my father helped us turn the seats into a bed, but I didn't sleep. I saw the lights drifting past outside, and the sky at night. I remember a tunnel, at least one. And the border controls. By morning we were in Italy. My sister and I had to sit on our suitcases while my father exchanged money. We were hungry. In a train station we were given milk with coffee and cookies. Now we're in Italy, my father said. You don't speak German any more. And yet we children didn't speak Italian. First we travelled to Mantua. To our uncle. He had already landed my father a job. Now I work in the carousel factory, my father said, and my sister and I didn't believe him. Take us with you sometime, we begged him. Later we found out it was a soft drink factory. The three of us slept in the living room. In the evenings we watched the adults play cards. And we watched every week my father hand over a cut of his pay. They always argued over how much he would keep for himself. We had to pretend to sleep, otherwise the argument certainly would have got worse. My father hid the money left him between layers of clothing, still in his suitcase. He always acted as if he were putting it in a small interior side pocket of the suitcase, but in reality it was in a summer shirt that he never wore. I saw that. But it was nice in Mantua, all things considered. On the weekends we drove to the Po, with other families. Sometimes children from our school came along as well. At first they laughed at me and my sister, but once we could speak the language they stopped. The women lay in the sun. We played. Sometimes the men went fishing. We ate in the shadows of trees, poplars I think. Once I found a worm in my cheese, but at first I thought it only the shadow of one of the small fluttering leaves above me. When the schoolyear ended we went to the valley, to my grandmother's. *Up there*, we heard more and more frequently in the weeks prior. Up there in the valley. As if we were crossing into another country. My father bought a car. It was old and a bit dinged up, but that's how all the cars were there. My aunt cried when we left, but I think they were relieved when we drove off. In the valley everything changed. Mantua had been an intermediate country, now we were in a new world. My grandmother always wore black dresses, I never saw her in anything else. She was a thin woman, but very strong. She lifted huge blocks of wood in front of the shed and split them with an axe as if they were apples. She spoke the local language; we did not understand it, but quickly grasped the important things. She pointed, for example, up at the mountain, grabbing hold of our necks so we could do nothing but look at it. At the time I thought the bare chalk cliffs were snow.

Summer was long. We had to help a lot, in the small fields before the village. Potatoes, garlic, carrots, cabbage. Beans. The garlic and the potatoes were the most important. And the pig. The pig was miserable. It lived in a hovel below the house; in the wall there was a small portal just large enough for the small feeding trough. One saw the pig's snout, and nothing else, until it was slaughtered. When it was alive no one loved the pig, but when it was dead they loved it all the more so. Such a pig has to keep for a long time, all winter. Every part of it was eaten, aside from the bristles. In winter there was bean soup with the grey, soft fat from the pig's belly. When my grandmother caught me spitting the pieces of fat into my hand in order to give them to the dog, without saying a word she stood up and lifted her hand, which was all bones, and gave me a flat blow to the back of my neck, and I had to put the pieces of meat back in my bowl. The pig, or more accurately pigs – since there was a new one every year – those pigs taught me a lot. The way they gobbled and gobbled, only to be eaten. Our house had considerable damages from the earthquake, but in my memory we didn't have a pig yet, it was only May. Walls caved in and ceilings collapsed, and the small pig hovel was buried: that would have been the pig's end. You could hear the pigs shrieking in other houses, the shriek high-pitched and piercing and breathless, and no one could help them because the hovels were buried beneath rubble. Of course everyone tried to rescue their pig, but it took time, and the people were more important, after all. I believe some pigs even died of fright.

COMMON GLIDER
The common glider appears in May. It is as if its wings were made of matte rust with white markings – a stripe of small pseudo-feathers. The butterfly glides and hovers in the air, landing only briefly on leaves, staying away from flowers. The caterpillar bears golden dapples, which transform into the pseudo-feathers as it sleeps, metamorphizing in its chrysalis.

GIGI
Here in the valley, most important things are white. The stone, the garlic, the goats. And in winter, the snow. In the past they also fired limestone in the forests. The old limekilns occasionally stand in our way when we fell

trees. They are ruins now, but it wasn't that long ago. The older people here still knew the ins and outs. Which stones from the brooks and rivers are suited, which boulders from the fresh landslides. The fired limestone was brought down into the valley, all the way to Udine, where it was sold. Today you're better off avoiding the limekilns. Vipers live inside them, in the hollow centres. I've seen it myself.

Today there's no money in stone. Only in wood. For building, for heating. For furniture. I'm only involved in cutting timber. In the forest I know my way around. And aside from that, in the barn. With the goats. Milking, making cheese. Mucking stalls. Goats are very sensitive. And then the young arrive. Usually in May. But back then, in the earthquake year, they didn't. Now I can't remember why. Goats are good mothers. When you take away the bucklings for the slaughter, the mothers cry for one day and one night. You can never slaughter a buckling where its mother will hear it scream. May she think it was merely taken away, I say to myself. May she think this, and not hear how it screams.

I was always good with goats. The goats have chosen you, the others would say. I milked and took care of and minded them. Goats are clever animals, but they eat whatever they find. Then they struggle with colic. Once we had a buckling stay at our place past slaughtering time – maybe no one had bought it; at some point we must have slaughtered it ourselves. If a buck lives among the nannies, the milk stinks, that's just how it is. The cheese will also turn spicy and buckish. The buckling had eaten alfalfa at the edge of the field, and it lay there, its stomach so swollen I thought it would explode. But the buckling recovered. Goats are also sensitive to the insane. A few houses above ours lived an insane woman. Sometimes she laughed for hours, such a screeching, shrill laugh. You could hear right away that she was not amused. It started the same every time; I can still hear it: Hahahahaha. The same every time. Five times, *ha*. The first and third *ha* higher and louder than the other three. If she laughed a lot, something would go wrong with the milk, I could swear. The milk quickly soured, and the cheese didn't turn out. Laughing cheese, that's what I called this failed cheese. I often sat around the barn with the goats and talked to them. Among people I was never a big talker, but with the goats I was. In summer when we didn't fell timber sometimes I stayed up in the meadow for days. It was my mountain pasture. Eventually I installed a simple milk kitchen and built myself a bed, and there was a fire pit outside. Those were the most wonderful times. When you stood there and looked up at Canin, it was as if you could walk directly from the meadow onto the scree-covered hillside below the peak, and from there up to the ridge. But that was an illusion. Below the peak snow lay into the summer. I never went that high up in the mountains, where nothing more grows and not a tree stands. Only stone. I went only as far as the goats did. Sometimes I saw someone ascending. Mountain climbers, bootleggers, people crossing the border – after all, it was just on the other side. One autumn the Alpini came to train, allegedly climbing to the top of Canin, but I didn't see it; I was already back in the village, with the goats. Once I saw a landslide. A small avalanche of scree. I even heard the rumble. In the mountains something is always shifting.

Yes, I was chosen by the goats, so I also helped when they had their young. Once a goat struggled. I reached in with my hand and felt two kids inside. The first one lay so crooked and askew that I had to break its neck in order to get it out. That's something I'll never forget: how it felt to my hand. I pulled it out, and then the second one came, and the mother goat survived. I washed my arm, scrubbed it, but for days it smelled of blood, and at night I could not sleep, I felt the small bones forever breaking in my hand. To this day my arm itches, above all at night; then I scratch it, for hours sometimes. That's why my arm is covered in scars.

TONI

A few houses in the village had gardens. The rest of us all had our fields for corn and vegetables and potatoes outside the village, a strip each. There was a cherry tree in one garden – I still remember it. The cherries were small and bitter, but the owner always covered the tree with a net, after the blossoms fell off, to protect his cherries. Once a bird became trapped in it – that was shortly before the earthquake. It was a small bird, greenish yellow, with a bit of brown or black, like the greenfinches many people kept in cages. It was a siskin, the man with the tree said. A Eurasian siskin, a bird that frequents alders. On one of its legs the bird had a ring. The man brought it to my father to help him hold the bird still, so he could read what was written on the ring. The bird was terrified, it shat on my father's finger, and I feared my father would squeeze it to death. Then the ring suddenly detached, and the bird slipped away from my father. According to the ring, the bird was from Moscow, my father claimed. He even read it out, in order to demonstrate that he could read Russian letters. I felt bad for the bird; I hope it was able to build itself a nest. There are enough alders around here. It flew from Moscow to us in the valley. I wondered if there were alders in Moscow, between all the houses. Of all places, it had flown to us – I could hardly believe it.

MARA

I've always been fond of birds. Ever since I was a child. My father could imitate bird calls like no other. He brought me along to the forest, and made me shut my eyes. We listened to the birds. I learned the call of the Eurasian jay and the nuthatch and all the various tits, as well as the serin and the greenfinch. Then I had to say if the call came from my father or from an actual bird. I peeked through my fingers and watched as he stood there stiffly, angling his head or sticking it out in front of him, pursing his lips or rounding them. Occasionally I laughed, but he never noticed; most of the time he had his eyes closed himself. Then I always said: That was a bird! And he would be pleased. Really? He would ask. You sure? Yes, I'm sure, I would say, and he would stroke the top of my head. You'll learn to do it soon, too, he always promised. Today I'm not sure if I really sound like a bird.

My father could also imitate birds I had never heard here in the valley. Above all the oriole. He had heard it further out, where the plains already begin. Past Venzone you'll hear it, he said. In summer we occasionally drive to Venzone and walk there in the forest. I'm not able to imitate the call any more, but it went straight to my heart whenever my father did. I still remember him telling me that orioles call out to one another for hours, as if searching for one another.

My father had binoculars, which we brought along whenever we climbed higher up. His binoculars were from the war, he had been a mountain infantryman. He was very proud of them. Whenever he picked up his binoculars, he said: They were a reward for my bravery. But my mother was of the opinion that he had simply stolen them. Or helped himself to them – that's how she put it.

Whenever we went into the mountains, up and up past

the last town, I too was allowed to look through the binoculars. While scanning the rock, rifts and nicks appeared where with a naked eye the mountains had looked totally smooth, and you could see sparse meadows and small trees, and once I saw a mountain climber. A very small figure, but I saw it clearly, their backpack. I wanted to show my father but he couldn't find the figure, and when I looked through the binoculars again it was gone. It's not easy to make out what's what in the world through binoculars; all around there are only individual pieces and even the colours are different.

Sometimes we saw alpine choughs. Alpine choughs are trusting birds, they flew around us as if wanting to become acquainted. I also learned their call, which is such a chirrupish sharp call – not like crows, friendlier. Eventually I was able to attract alpine choughs with my call.

I always spent a lot of time in the forest, even later, without my father. I would sit down on a tree stump and listen for the birds I knew. Then I would try to imitate them. The coal tit and the chaffinch and the nuthatch. I've always adored the nuthatch, its penetrating call; it's more of a warning or a search call than a song. Sometimes I felt they answered me. But I also always looked around to make sure no one was nearby. I didn't want to be observed. The bird calls were my secret. Later, when my mother became so disoriented and was often so restless at night, I sat with her and imitated the birds; it calmed her down, sometimes she even smiled. Her favourite was the alpine chough.

In the village many people kept birds in cages: canaries, greenfinches, siskins. Caged birds always sing with such a melancholy air, and people like that. Birds sense all great things in nature, expressing it in their songs, but it's always sad. Windstorms, thunderstorms and even the earthquake. If one had learned the language of the birds they would have known the earthquake was coming. But they still wouldn't have been able to do anything about it.

And what became of all the birds? Did they perish? Were they set free? Certainly some of them set themselves free, if the birdcage shattered or the small door opened in the earthquake's blows. They would have been disoriented, surely afraid, too, on the dark evening with all that noise. They didn't have nests to return to. And afterwards, while cleaning up and establishing order, people hung the empty birdcages in the windows, the small doors left open, as if to lure the birds back from their freedom. But I can't imagine any bird would want to move back into a cage. Maybe they all quickly adjusted to the wilderness, except the canaries – they aren't native, so they must have died, especially once the cold hit. But the others, the greenfinches and the siskins, they might have returned to the wild. Maybe they also recognized other birds, who knows. For them it was a joyful return to their native habitat. And they certainly sang differently – brighter, happier, not as full of melancholy as when in the cage. It is the cage that makes their song so beautiful and sad. That's a strange relationship – and also strange that humans take advantage of it, the connection between the sadness of captivity and beautiful song.

WINTER ROSE

The winter rose burgeons under the snow and is the first flower to arrive after winter, still without colour in its blossoms, which are a greenish white, as if unfinished in their colour, although the form is beautiful and bell-like and has nothing unfinished about it. The roots of the winter rose make one sneeze – it clears the head, they say – and boiled as a stock it will straighten out a mad person's head, above all women suffering from childbed fever. For this the roots have to be cut during the full moon and immediately set to simmer. Whoever drinks winter rose broth purges her madness in the form of a black liquid. She is struck thereupon by a great weakness that leads to her recovery. Winter roses grow in light forests, having a predilection for slopes, and are often found near early white anemones and wild pink columbines.

LINA

The soil is poor here. Limestone ground, the ground of poverty. The flowers are paler here than elsewhere. The winter is long. But winter is alright by us, because it brings snow and whatever grows around here has snow and goat shit to thank for it. The snow saturates the ground differently than the rain does, they always say. On the other side of the mountain, in the south, it only rains, even in winter no snow falls. It's God's pisser, the people say.

What is my life? sometimes I ask myself. My life is this place. Here I know everything. Every stick and every stone. The animals and the people. I write down what I want to remember. The weather, the harvest, the comings and goings, misfortunes. Surprises. I have three garlic fields. They aren't large; one is behind the cemetery, one is further below on the hillside, halfway to the river, one is behind the house. For these fields I need no help. Planting, weeding, thinning, harvesting, I do it all by myself. I also have rabbits. A dozen. A whole row of little hutches. No one can slaughter a rabbit as fast as I do. In seconds. Open the door, grab hold of the rabbit, always by its neck, tightly. The knife has to be very sharp, but that's what the knife grinders are there for. Nowhere are the knives as sharp as they are here. Slit its throat, bleed it dry, skin it. Around here we eat a lot of rabbits, it isn't expensive. Every time I see the animals skinned and gutted and hanging upside down from a hook, I think they look like malevolent, dangerous, snappish creatures. Like rats, only larger. Every time it's such a strange metamorphosis. Rabbits, of all animals.

My husband works abroad. First he was in Switzerland for a year building roads, now he's a waiter in Germany. Every few months he comes home. Then it's time to work on the house, repair things, cut wood. That's how it always was here. Poverty sends people packing, longing brings them back. But it also breeds bitterness. When my husband comes home, he's like a stranger, it takes a week or two for everything to be okay again, but then he's soon gone.

ERYNGO
Eryngo is a native thistle. In late summer the umbels turn a silvery blue. At twilight the blossoms glow wanly among the limestone. Eryngo is a flower of unfertile landscapes. It commits itself to the ground, which, as if to commemorate this withered, faded, and scattered thistle, lets nothing else grow in its place.

SILVIA
Something else occurred to me, although I can't be sure when it happened, if it was on the day of the earthquake, or the day before. At any rate it was hot. Wasps had begun building a nest below the ledge of the window facing the yard. More than once in summer the wasps would

swarm out to build their nest. This year they came early. They buzzed so loudly that we heard it all the way in the house. One stung me on my elbow as I walked by. A wasp sting is very painful, but it's over in no time if you put a slice of onion on it. I stood at a distance from the window and pressed the onion onto the sting. In the corner between window ledge and masonry wall there already hung a ball, full of holes. It was brownish, as if made of adobe. The wasps hung from it and whirred about. That afternoon my grandmother told me to knock off the ball. I was afraid, the wasps might become angry. Everyone knows how furious a swarm of wasps can become. I took the longest stick I could find, a stick from the shed – in summer we needed them for the beans. I stuck the tip of it into the nest; immediately it fell to the ground. I ran into the house, but the wasps remained utterly still. Inside I couldn't hear them at all. From the kitchen window I could see a few of them landing on it and taking off, as if disoriented. My grandmother sent me outside, to bring the stick back to the shed. Once I had put away the stick I saw the nest lying on the ground. It almost looked like a skull. It wasn't a ball, but rather oblong. The holes looked like eyes. A few small wasps were stuck in the corner beneath the window ledge. They didn't buzz, only rubbed their front legs together, as if they were freezing, crowding close together in a small group. They were the children, tucked snugly already in the nest, I thought. I felt bad for them. I never checked on them again, though, because the earthquake came, either that evening or the following evening. I had forgotten the wasp nest. But I remember it now. It must have been one of those hot days in May.

Once we had a hornets' nest in the gable – that had to stay. Chasing away hornets brings bad luck, my grandmother said. There's no reason to be afraid of them. They always stuck together, and occasionally in the evening one would fly against the illuminated window. Sometimes I climbed up to the attic and listened out for their buzzing from the inside. It was like music, I could listen to it for so long. Once in the act of this I found a tiny dead shrew up there. Who knows how it got in there, so alone; maybe it was the cat. The shrew was entirely dry and rattled quietly if you took it by the tail and moved it. It almost sounded like a rattling, that's how dry it was.

BIRD UNKNOWN

With the earthquake rain set in, followed by snow. The snow lay wet and heavy on the May meadows. At the edge of one meadow, the Alpini, who had brought relief aid, found in the snow a dead bird with outstretched wings, as if it had met disaster and fallen from the clouds. It was a large bird, and its feathers, appearing black at first, proved – in a sudden burst of sunshine – to be a variously shaded blue, shining iridescent between purple and green on the underside of its wings. The head was larger and rounder than that of a raven, and the dark red beak was formed from thick, wattle-like pockets that began directly below its eyes. No one had ever seen a bird like this and no one knew how to classify it, they knew no other bird to compare it to, nor to what taxonomic order it belonged, and thus knew not how to name it generally. So they called it *bird unknown*, and sent the group of children, who had stood, all curiosity, around them as they racked their brains, to bury it in a quiet place where no wild animal might root it up.

III

'At length, as the destruction of the outer envelope of the earth extends deeper, there stand revealed the elongated cicatrices, and those great swollen cake-like masses of intrusive granite or syenite, which bring about the metamorphosis of the sedimentary beds forming their roof; and by these we are put upon the trail of a series of great abyssal phenomena.

These phenomena seem to stand in some causal connection with the absence of the tangential component in the dislocations of our mountains – with the passive subsidence of extensive plates and great fragments of the crust into the profound depths below.'
— Eduard Suess, *The Face of the Earth*, vol. 1 (1892)

WHITE AND BLACK

The white river also includes a black river. This is how the world is ordered: into the white north and the black south. Ice and cinders. Limestone and bitumen. The Rio Nero is a brook that stretches a few kilometres, originating from the wall of violet-grey mountains that separate the valley from the hill landscape and after it, the plain. Thus walled off, so rocky and fissured, in the valley any possibility of a plain, of a bright white and ruling sky, is lost. Seen from the valley it is a raw chain of cliffs with occasional shims of forest shoving their way into the heights, against the paler shims of avalanches. At sunrise it all appears very pliant and soft, the fissures and fractures in the stone, the transitions from forest to field, the soft cupolas of treetops. A boundary as found in fairy tales, which calls into question all knowledge about territory and terrain, letting a yonder vibrate in all possible colours and grades of light, the question of what is real arising again and again.

Up the Rio Nero, the terrain is always wild. The path is forever being shifted by fresh rock falls and descending scree – a terrain of interference in the tenor of events. The scent of resin sits above the sunny barren land, where dwarf pines brace themselves between chunks of rock – the trees so small one might be quicker to attribute to the stones their scent. Beside the pine saplings junipers take root, small bell flowers, heather on blown-in soil.

The path leads steeply uphill past white-grey rock faces, through sparse conifers, through a quiet, shady, still beech grove protected from wind. Again and again one encounters the brook – where it drops from great heights it forms small sparkling lakes before falling further down. Few songbirds to be heard, occasionally birds of prey calling out, sharp and brief. Here and there it is impassable, simply left open to the hiker – to labour, using hands and knees and feet on the rocks, to feel for their own path to climb, to scrape and scratch their skin, leaving behind thin traces of blood. In summer you have to be on guard for snakes, for the rushing quiet, broken by the trickle of distant scree. Rio Nero is bright and white and, like all mountain brooks, greenish where it forms deeper pools, never broad. At some point the path leaves the brook's course, without ever having reached its source, and in an arc leads to the mountain pasture at the foot of Monte Cuzzer. If it weren't for the beech grove just crossed and the group of high moor ferns that followed it, the small plateau with the hut would seem inescapable, sitting tight between rugged mountain faces. The narrow paths from south and north up to the peak are barely distinguishable: scree ways, with a dry drumming of fallen rocks waiting at every step. Once reached, the apex is an incision between two worlds. On one side, the valley, chalk-white and tree-green, heading for Monte Canin, barred and harsh; on the other side, a country that dissipates in light, inaccessible behind falling chains of rock, facing the foreign shimmering strip – a hint of horizon. Once on the crest one ceases to believe that the Rio Nero could carry anything from this bright, foreign country south of the mountains into the valley.

ANSELMO

The gravel quarry in Germany was not far from the house where we lived. Only the pub and the lorry park lay between them. That's where the route already split off to the quarry. I can still see it in my mind's eye. The road, unpaved and after every rain full of puddles. When I couldn't sleep at night I would listen to the gravel chute, which stood beside the piles of excavated sand and dirt. A massive funnel with pipes that the stones – organized according to size – slid down, forming pointy hills. At all times the sound of stone, this rolling. The sound persisted all night, or so it seems to me now when I think back on it, although that can't be possible. The hills of gravel and sand stood like a wreath around the edge of the quarry, which – shaped like a funnel itself – grew ever smaller towards the bottom. At the very bottom was a small lake: round, located precisely in the middle. The way down to the watering hole was marked by deep tyre marks from the trucks. Down in the quarry they only loaded sand.

The quarry was forbidden to us. No one was allowed to go there. When the workers went home they blocked the entrance with a chain, and a sign that read: Parents are responsible for their children. I didn't know what that meant. I asked my mother, but she always said: *dumb question*, whenever she didn't know the answer. A lot of children played in the gravel quarry anyway, when the guards weren't there. They drilled holes into the walls and talked about underground passages. Once a cave collapsed when a child was inside it. But I didn't see that happen. Only later, when the police and the fire department came. An ambulance arrived, it was getting dark and the entire street flickered blue. We looked out the window. The child's mother came running down the street, straight for the gravel quarry. I think there was even a helicopter. The next day at school they said the boy was dead. Suffocated. He had gone to our school. After that I always thought of him at night when I heard the gravel chutes.

LINA

I'm the middle child. There are five of us. I have two older
brothers, two younger sisters. I grew up in the post-war
years. We weren't poor and we weren't rich either. Each of
us had our own bed. In winter there was always a fire in
the woodstove. My father worked for the postal service,
outside the valley. We had enough to eat. When I was
young I would sit outside next to my grandmother on the
little bench, and she would tell me the names of all the
mountains. There was a story for each name. And in each
story there was a misfortune. In these tales it was always
as if the people sat, grafted onto the white stone of these
mountains and hillsides, just waiting for their misfortune.
Don't tell the child those scary stories, my mother would
say, but my grandmother would ignore her. To this day
whenever I sit in front of our house I think: That's where
the hunter fell into a rock crevice, he who always calls
out in a storm; there a bolt of lightning hit a pair of lovers
gone lost in the mountains, they became ashes washed
away by the rain and blown off by the wind, only their
hands remaining, burned into the stone. And the shadow
there by the *bábe*, that's the *Venedigermandl,* the little old
Venetian man, the dwarf who grows as tall as a giant when
a storm brews. Like this, her stories are all laid out before
me, written into the landscape. As she aged she became
smaller and smaller, my grandmother, and at some point
her hands were like those of a child, yet bony and spotted, whereas children's hands are soft. My lass, she always
said to me, my lass, beware of Dujak – that is the spirit we
believe in here – at night he haunts the village, and she
whispered to me about the Huda Ura, the thunderstorm
witch, and Morá, who comes to take people from life into
death. I was already grown up but still sat with my grandmother on the bench, and it was as if the situation were

97

inverted: now she was the little one perched beside me and I was big and held her precious hand, though can such a small, bony hand really be precious? She told me about Riba Faronika, the mermaid who started the earthquake with her cloven fishtail.

Your brother is a *hallodri*, she would often say, referring to the younger of my brothers, who was always fighting with father and his older brother. He's bound to bring misfortune on us all, she said, but I laughed; I still loved him, my brother. But in the end she proved right: it was spring, Canin was still covered in snow and it was exceptionally clear, you could see every small fissure in the stone, and there was something, a shadow, a gust of wind, a dark cloud, and my small grandmother said: If only we get through the day without misfortune!

My brother went that evening to the neighbouring village – there was a girl there he was crazy about – and a fight broke out. He came home in the middle of the night, I heard him, and he whispered with my mother, They'll be here any minute, any minute now, he cried like a child, and my mother packed a few things for him and he left, without saying goodbye. He was just gone and my mother didn't say a word about it for weeks, it was as if he'd never existed. Later it came out that he thought he'd beaten someone to death in a fight, and he just ran away, through the forest, gone. Probably to Udine. And then he got a job abroad. At some point a postcard arrived from Germany. Finding work abroad was easy. Everyone wants to go to Germany, to Switzerland, to the wealthy countries. In general a lot of people have gone. All the way to Argentina. They had to go, there wasn't enough work around here. That's how it always was. So it wasn't a misfortune, as my grandmother would have had it. It was a good thing. Good because he no longer fought with our older brother, good that he thought he had beaten to death someone who lived after all, good that he went to Germany. On the postcard was a castle, a castle and a forest, but the forest was entirely unlike ours. Maybe it only looked different because the postcard was black-and-white. Later he sometimes sent presents, above all for my mother. He was still gone when my grandmother died. Once he came to visit, bragging about his German girlfriends and passing around little photographs. Later he returned for good. He already drank a lot then. He had forgotten how to sing and dance, and once when he was very drunk he told me about how he had got someone pregnant in Germany, and that was the only reason he'd come back.

When I sit outside and look at the mountains, I place my hand on the bench and it is as if my grandmother's tiny, old, bony child's hand were beneath it. She had always spoken of misfortune, but she was dead a long time before the earthquake finally came.

THE PHARAONIC FISH

According to the creation narrative, water and land were separated, and the soil was made fecund on the third day – before the division of light and darkness, before the division of day and night and before their alternation, which first introduced the concept of time: the nameable dimension of transience.

And before the division of day and night, as the myth of Riba Faronika would have it, God stood at the edge of the land freshly separated from the sea, and bent down to the newly revealed dry material, which here on this shore was sand. He took a handful of sand and threw it into the water. And a grain of sand from God's hand, but a single one, landed on the back of Riba Faronika, the pharaonic fish. As graceful as she was powerful, named after an event that had not yet happened and at the same time was already inside her, Riba Faronika's belly, as if the future were decided in her belly, specifically the event of the Red Sea: a terrific wind, like the prelude to an earthquake, divided the Red Sea in two, allowing the Israelites, who were fleeing the pharaonic soldiers, to walk on dry ground to safety. And the soldiers who stormed after the Israelites and went under in the waves of the Red Sea once the waters closed are said to have all become pharaonic fish, their human upper bodies equipped below with a cloven fishtail.

The Riba Faronika of this story of the world's creation nevertheless slumbered deep in the sea, a powerful creature with a woman's body down to her belly, and a cloven fishtail below it. Startled by the grain of sand, she flicked her fish tail, and the Earth rumbled and folded into mountains in every direction. And marvelling at the rumbling that she had caused, Riba Faronika turned around, and the ocean flooded the Earth, and as she withdrew, the dry land separated into continents.

Riba Faronika lies sleeping, deep at the bottom of the ocean, but from time to time she flicks her fish tail in a dream, and parts of the earth move.

SILVIA

My mother is not from the valley. She scooped up your father down there, my grandmother would say. Down there meant in the flatlands, before the valleys, before the mountains. By the sea. My father was on the road as a knife grinder. A lot of people from our village travelled as knife grinders. A few weeks at a time, everyone had their

100

own zone. Our neighbour went all the way to Bologna. My father travelled to the seaside. Lignano, Bibione. Jesolo. Occasionally he went inland, to Pordenone, Codroipo. These names remain in my memory. I haven't seen all the places myself, but I can remember the names. From somewhere around there he brought my mother. My father continued working as a travelling knife grinder, always with Sergio, an older man from our village. He would be gone for weeks. When he came back he would work on the house, cut wood, slaughter the pig, fell trees in the forest. Once he accidentally drove an axe into his shin. The other men brought him to the village on a stretcher made from sticks, his pant leg soaked in blood. The bar owner drove him to the hospital. He couldn't work for a long time and limped around the house. They were always arguing. Until my mother said: Now I'm going to get a job. She packed her bags and drove to the shore. Once a week she called the bar and the owner would come get us. She found a job, as a waitress, I think. I'm doing well, she always said, I'm doing well, I'm at the seaside. What should I bring you? I never knew how to answer. What should I have said? By the time she came she would have forgotten what I wanted anyway. She didn't come often. But she always brought me something. Beautiful dresses. Once it was a pair of pink sandals that fit me only for a month. And a red bag that I could hang on my shoulder, I still have it today.

It was nice when she visited. Like a holiday. She would stay a few days, then they would start to argue.

My mother smoked a lot. She dressed elegantly in high heels, and stood there like that, smoking. Sometimes she was called to answer the phone in the bar, then she took off her high heels and ran off barefoot.

Don't be so smug, my father sometimes yelled. Then

she took her cigarettes and went to bed. She continued to smoke there. Sometimes she sang pop songs. She sang 'Piccolo uomo', she especially liked that one, and as she sang she walked back and forth, a cigarette in her hand. Like in a film. She sang beautifully, like a real pop singer. It made my father angry. Once my mother stood, as she often did, at the window and smoked. My father was eating. My grandmother had made polenta. Down there they call me Patty Pravo, my mother said. The men, too? my father asked. Yes, the men, too, she answered. Then my father jumped up and hit her with the polenta spoon. He was still limping. My mother packed her suitcase and rode off on the bus. Very early in the morning. I heard her shoes on the street. I loved my mother very much, but that time I was happy she left.

ANSELMO

After the earthquake everything was in a state of chaos. We had a car, the children slept inside it. Many people were afraid to enter their houses, even when they appeared to be in one piece, but our house was destroyed, we couldn't have slept in it at all. At night my sister and I spoke in German about our mother, and about how she might have thought us dead. We spoke in German so the other children wouldn't understand. I lay in the car and imagined that I really was dead. Later I wished I had been one of the ones they pulled out from under the rubble. It was a big commotion, people clapped and cried.

I don't remember exactly when the Alpini came, but that changed everything. The first men arrived in helicopters, bringing blankets and food and search-and-rescue dogs, in case people were still buried under the rubble. But around us in the village everyone was accounted for, so the soldiers with dogs got back into the helicopter and flew on to another village, where everything was much worse, that's what we heard.

The next group of soldiers came with trucks, after streets were cleared. They had to roll a massive boulder into the river. The soldiers pitched tents and built a kitchen, and later they also helped clear away the rubble, but not until they could bring in the backhoes. We children always trailed them and watched. We still had school, as well, outside or in the tent, all of us together, but there were no proper lessons. Many children said that their school things had disappeared or been buried. We sang and talked and did mental arithmetic.

That summer I learned to catch vipers. Suddenly I wasn't afraid any more at all. I was always the first to spot them, too. Occasionally we went on a hunt, everyone wanted to catch a viper. At the pharmacy there was money to be made with vipers. At least there had been in other years, before the earthquake: the pharmacy was in the chief village, where many houses were destroyed. This much for a dead viper and this much for a live one. Live ones were worth more. I practised all summer, and I became very good. Once I brought a captured viper in a jar to the soldiers. At first they didn't believe I had caught it. The viper sat at the bottom of the jar and was afraid. Maybe it still hoped to get out. Bravo! said the Alpini. Just don't let it out, then it will want revenge! I couldn't bring it to the pharmacy, so I hid the jar behind the rubble in front of our house vestibule. Later when I went to get it, it was gone. Once our house stood again, occasionally I was seized by fear: the viper was somewhere inside, between the stones. Vipers are very powerful, in spring they push their way out of the stony ground, out of the cliffs.

The summer after the earthquake was beautiful, or at

least the beginning was. My father didn't pay attention to us. He was constantly building and repairing things around the house, so we could move back in. Who wanted to keep living in a tent? Aside from children, perhaps. He also helped other people; people whose houses had major damages helped one another for as long as they could, or until there was an argument. There was always an argument eventually. We children were suddenly invisible and no one smacked us – only once, when we built a fire. My sister and I built fires often; once an embankment caught fire and people ran over to put it out, and my grandmother asked us if we had lit it, smacking us on the back of the neck, but we didn't say a word, and afterwards people blamed it on a fool who lumbered in every few weeks, panhandling. That was before the earthquake. In the weeks after the earthquake we certainly had it good, as did the other children, no one was smacked. Eventually a packet arrived from my mother, full of clothes and shoes and gummy bears. She knew, after all, that we weren't dead.

TALE OF THE SHIRT

A tale of the region goes like this:

Out in the plains there lived a prince who was always sad. He was so sad that he no longer wanted to live. His mother tried everything she could to lift his spirits, but nothing helped. Eventually she brought in a doctor: he examined the prince, tickled him, sang cheerful songs and told him jokes, but nothing assuaged the prince's sadness.

Only one thing can help him, the doctor told the prince's mother. You have to find a happy person, and bring him their shirt.

Without delay, the mother set off in search of a happy person. After she had been out for nearly an entire day she met a shepherd, who played his flute so sweetly as he wandered among his sheep. Are you happy? The prince's mother asked him.

The shepherd answered, Absolutely, my sheep are brave and my flute is beautiful. Why do you ask?

My son, the prince, is very sad and the doctor says he will recover from his sadness only if he is given a happy person's shirt.

Well, okay, said the shepherd, I'll trade you for that handsome hat!

You can't be that happy, after all, said the mother of the prince, if you demand something in exchange.

She continued on her journey, the sun was already low in the sky, and she met a winegrower, leaving his vineyard, where he had just raked the furrows between the vines. He whistled a tune to himself and the prince's mother asked him at once: Are you happy?

As ever! the winegrower answered. My life is good, and so is my wine. Why do you ask?

My son, the prince, is very sad and the doctor says he will recover from his sadness only if he is given a happy person's shirt.

And how many gold pieces will you give me for it? the winegrower asked.

You can't be that happy, after all, said the prince's mother, if you demand gold pieces in exchange.

Then she reached a valley. The mountains towered all around, and down the middle flowed a river, full of large stones. Behind a large boulder she heard someone knocking stones, singing at the top of his lungs all the while. She couldn't understand the words, but it sounded merry.

Stone carver! she called out. Are you happy?

She had to call out three times before he heard her.

How could I not be happy! he called back. The sun is warm, the water cool!

Stone carver, my son, the prince, is very sad and the doctor says he will recover from his sadness only if he is given a happy person's shirt. Give me your shirt – then he'll be happy!

But I don't have a shirt! the stone carver called out, and his laugh was so loud and cheerful it echoed off the mountains.

MARA

At one time the fiddle maker was the most important man in the valley. Master of the *zitira*. Only boys play *zitira*. That was an unspoken rule. The men fiddled, the women sang. Dancing was done by all. My father was an important musician in the village. And he knew everything about wood. He could tell you: This wood is right for a *zitira*, this wood is best for a *bunkula*, this wood is for a stool, for musicians to sit on. He only played when he was in the mood; the rest of the time you could ask and beg as much as you pleased but it didn't matter, he wouldn't pick up his fiddle. When he did play, everyone wanted to listen, and before long someone would show up with a *bunkula*, and they would make music into the night. Once he said to me: I'll teach you how to play the *zitira*. I was thrilled, and I could already picture myself holding a *zitira* – the only girl to do so – but then he disappeared. He went into the mountains, and later they said he must have remained there, buried beneath an avalanche. Avalanches were common: the rock is weak, and now and again there are small seismic shocks and tremors that are hardly perceptible, yet perhaps recognizable by the behaviour of animals, or because there are several rockfalls within a short amount of time, or infrequently because of a light trembling under one's feet or a rattling of the window panes. Once a pitcher suddenly fell from the shelf; we all sat at the table, and the shelf was clattering, and the pitcher fell to the ground, just barely missing my father's head. That's a sign, my mother said – she was always angry at him. You just better watch out, that's a sign! Then she got up and swept up the shards. As she did, a small roll of bills appeared: I saw it clearly, the way my mother stuck it in the arm of her shirt, without saying a word. My father sat with his back to her. In any event, the day after his departure there was a fresh avalanche on Canin, visible from our house. But no one went looking for him. It was autumn, the weather turned bad. We don't really know anyway, they said back then – after all, he knows his way around the mountain. Later they said he must have crossed the border to Yugoslavia. He did cross the border from time to time; we children weren't supposed to know about it, but we did anyway. He was looking for someone, they later said, and all kinds of stories came out, as if people had suddenly invented an entire life for my father. First he was a smuggler, then he wanted to kill the man who had killed his brother in the resistance, then they said he had another family over there. I don't know, I never will. I was a wartime child. My mother was alone with us. I can still remember the day my father suddenly appeared. A woman walked up the steps between the neighbours' houses, up to our door, Beppe is back! she called out. Your husband's returned! That was after the war. I still remember it precisely. The sun was shining. He wore heavy shoes that thundered on the wooden steps. And right away it was as if a king had arrived, he called all the shots. We had to get warm water, and soap

– the tub was in the yard – and afterwards he burned his clothing, and my mother had to help him. Then he took his fiddle from the cabinet and tuned it. His orders, and this kingly air – my mother couldn't yield to it, nor could my older siblings, whom he hit. That's how it was for a few years. Four, maybe five years, until one autumn father disappeared. My older brothers were always arguing with him; they did not accept my father's authority after surviving the war without him. I can't remember when they left, whether it was before or after he disappeared. One of my brothers definitely left before. For America, or Argentina. I can't remember. Then he lured the others after him. I never saw them again, aside from a photograph or two, enclosed in a letter. I wouldn't recognize them if I saw them on the street. They could come to the valley and sit at the bar or pass me by and I wouldn't recognize them, for they would be strangers.

LEGEND
On the bumpy ridge next to Canin – which appears so restless in the presence of the great mountain, in its bearing towards it: at times small and beggarly, at times nearly as high as Canin's peak – there are the two *bábe*. You can see clearly only two of them – the large *bába* and the middle one – and whoever is not able to get the right angle – because they go dizzy, are afraid of heights or simply ignorant about the ways of seeing in the mountains – they will never see the third one, the small *bába*, which anyway doesn't count. The two *bábe*, they are women. Petrified, evil-done. What might they have effected to deserve this petrification? To how many places did they send a man to waste away in the mountains? At least that is how the story goes. He was a small man, a *Venedigermandl* – a little old

Venetian man – as they say, further west: one of the dwarfs who found entrances into mountain crevices and narrow caves in this region of chasms known as *abissi*, in order to look for gemstones and gold. Gold is hardly imaginable in limestone, maybe the *bábe* hoped for a gemstone. Who knows who put that idea into their heads. No further details about any gemstones are known. When the little man emerged from the mountain, with or without a gemstone, and they refused him his promised wages, the conned dwarf – suddenly equipped with a magic wand – transformed them into cliffs. A punishment and a warning. Only: Why was their little sister also made a believer, if the legend refers only to the two? There is no answer. The *bábe* stand there all alone. Too steep, smooth, treacherous to be suitable for hiking. Impassable. In the right light and weather hunchbacked. Deprived of every redemption.

TONI

I still remember the day we got our car. It was red. My father drove it home. A red 500. All our neighbours came to see it. The women stood together, talking about how we could drive to the sea now. My mother said, Yeah, to the sea, and then she raised her apron to her face, as if ashamed. The men stood around the car with my father, touching it and beeping the horn; someone kicked the back tyre with the tip of their shoe. But no one could find fault with the car. On Sunday my father drove us all the way to Gemona. My mother put on a pretty dress, and we children had to comb our hair before leaving. The drive downhill into the valley seemed so long to me, and I became a bit nauseated. But below on the main road everything was fine. In Gemona we walked up to the cathedral, and from there my father pointed out the factory where he worked. Where is the sea, my mother asked, and he pointed in another direction, but the sea itself wasn't visible. It was still far away. Two hours or so, my father said, we'll do that in the summer. Afterwards we ate ice cream, and my mother looked at the shop window displays. On the way home a motorcycle passed us. My father beeped his horn and drove quicker, in order to pass the motorcyclist, and we children called out: faster, faster, faster! But we didn't succeed – the motorcyclist drove even faster himself, until he skidded on a curve and fell, and the motorcycle broke into pieces, scattering across the entire street. We stopped right behind him. We all screamed, you could already see the blood creeping out from under the man. My father ran off; he wanted to call an ambulance and alert the police, and my mother stood on the side of the road with us children, covering our eyes: Don't look, she repeated over and over, Don't look, but between her fingers I did look, and I saw blood. Other cars pulled up and stopped, and then the police came, along with my father. He had to explain what happened. Dead, one of the police officers said, he is dead. My father had to say his name and show his papers. It took a long time, and I was nauseated. My sister trembled and whimpered all the while, like a little dog. When we got home it was nearly dark. Luckily there was no damage to the front of our car, my father said on the drive back, otherwise they would have thought it was my fault. What luck.

OLGA

When the soldiers arrived a few days later, everyone rejoiced. The Alpini, the Alpini! they all cried. They came in heavily loaded trucks and military vehicles. There

110

were still earthquake tremors every day. They weren't that bad any more, but still. Occasionally you could hear a rockslide in the mountains, or a landslide, and it rumbled then as well. Some of the houses considered intact suddenly developed cracks, or revealed them just then. Our neighbour Luigi sat in front of his house, only a week before he had finished building an extension. The extension stood solid, but the rear part of it appeared buckled. Luigi just stared, didn't even talk to anyone. His two children always walked back and forth, carrying things; the shed was also in one piece, as was the barn. Their elderly grandmother was such a thin, bitter woman; she began to neatly stack the fallen rooftiles and knock mortar off the stones that had broken loose. The children were wild and ill-mannered; they had grown up without a mother, and you could always hear quarrelling in their house. Luigi had brought them back with him from Germany, they were his children. Lord knows if they're his, I heard the old woman say. I once saw her throw a brick at the girl. She missed.

We entered our house through the side door and searched for things, cleaned up, carried things out. My clothes were full of dust. Everything was full of dust. To this day sometimes I wake up in the middle of the night feeling as if my mouth were full of dust. The taste of mortar dust and chalk. Now I will suffocate, I think, now I am buried below the rubble and will suffocate. In my nose and in my mouth I still have this memory, as if it were embossed, and I can never be sure when it will awake. However that may be, something wakes it, sometimes while I'm sleeping, sometimes abruptly in the middle of the day, at work, while I'm watching television. But it always passes, and I don't suffocate.

In some places it rained inside. My father made an

effort at restacking the firewood. But every day it rumbled everything back around. The shed itself was even out of joint.

The soldiers set up a field kitchen of sorts, where they cooked food, and they erected tents. People immediately stormed the tents. Some families snatched up three tents right away. Before long there was bad blood. We got a tent on the edge, which was good, since it meant we didn't have neighbours on every side.

One of the soldiers took a liking to me; he was short and had black eyes. Too short for me, but he was nice. He always came around asking if he could help. Once he said: You're not from here, are you? I laughed and said no, I'm not: guess where I'm from! He thought about it for a moment and then said: Naples? I didn't like that. I'm not sure why, but I didn't want to be taken for a Neapolitan. I'm from Caracas, I said proudly, and he thought I said Carrara. Venezuela, I explained, but somehow it didn't get through. Afterwards he didn't come around that often and I saw him with a small, chubby girl. But that didn't bother me.

MUTE
One story of the valley concerns the goat witch. She lived below in the village, near the river, with her goats. She could not speak – she merely gurgled – but she sang beautifully, without words, just sweet melodies. That's how she bewitches the goats, turning both them and their milk very white, the people said. It is true: her goats ate the finest herbs and had the whitest fur and produced the whitest milk. If they bleated when led past a cowshed, the cow's milk would dry up, and its udder would become infected, the people said – but the goat witch just grinned,

as if nothing had happened. In order to teach her a lesson, one evening the dairy farmer slipped into her yard and slit one of her goats' throat. The blood flowing onto the soil in the yard was black. The people became afraid of the witch and set her house ablaze, but hardly did the fire roar before a strong wind came from the south, driving the flames and sparks to the upper village. Everything wooden caught fire, and only black stumps remained. The goat witch was up and away, and only sometimes, when a strong wind blew, did people think they heard her song up in the forest.

SILVIA

My father was always going on about a moped. He wanted a moped. Not a car, he never mentioned that. Every time he left on the knife grinder's bicycle he would say: Maybe I'll have enough money for a moped when I'm back. But then he had his accident in the forest, and my mother went to the seaside and worked. For a time there was no talk of mopeds, until my father left to grind knives. Sharpening scissors and knives, patching umbrellas and even repairing radios, he could do all that. Sometimes he said: I think I'll go work in a factory, too. Other people did roadwork in Switzerland. Whoever wants to make something of themselves goes away, my father said. Come on then, let's all go to the seaside, my mother replied, but my father just shrugged his shoulders. Further away, he said. To work. Abroad. Once a big shiny black car pulled into the village. The Argentinians are here, they said, the Argentinians came! The Argentinians were the tavern owner's brother and his wife. And their two children. It was winter, but there wasn't any snow yet. The car was so large it practically blocked the street in front of the bar.

The woman from Argentina wore a fur coat, and the girl had a light blue coat with a fur collar. Her brother walked around in a shirt and trousers that only came down to his knees, remember it was winter. His knees were entirely blue. They had bought the coats in Rome, my mother said – she still lived with us then. The tavern owner's brother hit the big time in Argentina, now he had purchased a car solely for their vacation in Italy. He smoked cigars. All day long he stood in front of the bar, talking to people and smoking cigars. It was summer in Argentina, and the children had a long break, but they were almost always inside the house. Once I saw them playing ball, on the square by the entrance to the village, where the bus stopped. The girl in her light blue coat and the boy in shorts. School let out at noon, a few children yelled something or wanted to play with them, but the two children just turned around without saying a thing, and went back into the bar. When the Argentinians left, my mother told me they were going skiing. In Switzerland. Or in Cortina, she said. Are these people somehow your business? my grandmother jumped down her throat. Just because they're lazy like you?

My mother and my grandmother couldn't stand each other. My father was stuck in the middle. He started saving money for a moped, he kept it in a coffee canister that was already beginning to rust. You've definitely got enough together for a wheel, my mum said when she was trying to provoke him, I'm not sure if she meant to be nasty. Either way, she left. When my father went back on the road to sharpen knives he took along the canister. And then he returned with the moped. He pushed, and I sat on the saddle, and I think he said: Now we can go visit mum at the sea. But that was the day of the earthquake, and I saw the moped buried beneath the rubble. At the time I thought my father was dead.

TONI

Many people left the village for work. Other children received presents from abroad in the mail, and a few also moved away, along with their mothers, to their fathers in Germany or Switzerland. A few had relatives in America or Argentina. My father's cousin, Luigi, returned with his kids – but not his wife. His German, my father called her. He forgot his German up there. The children didn't speak our language, but they learned Italian. Whenever they bickered they immediately threw punches. That girl is a wild animal, my mother said once, after witnessing her hit her brother. They never spoke of Germany. Their father had built a large carousel there, they said, a giant carousel with cars shaped like rockets that shot up in the air during the ride, higher than any tower. I didn't believe them, but kept my mouth shut. Once the carousel was finished they came to us in the valley. My father had a good job at the factory, and he was satisfied. Doing the same thing every day – it doesn't bother me, he said. But I always wanted to get out, I don't know why. *Out* above all, but I didn't want to go to Germany. My father was a communist, as was my grandfather before him, and we had an etched glass picture of a city with onion domes hanging in our window. That's Moscow, my father told everyone, we danced there. My father was in a folk dancing troupe. The people cheered for us, my father always said, when the conversation turned to his Russian trip. We received the greatest applause. I wanted to go to Russia, but not because my father had been there. At school I had seen photos of Moscow; our teacher had a large book lying around for anyone to look at, with pictures of massive buildings and broad avenues. Russian isn't difficult, our teacher said. Anyone who can speak our language will be speaking Russian in no time. A few of the photographs of Moscow were taken from an airplane, or at least from a great height. Buildings, buildings up to the horizon and not a hill in sight. Once, when Luigi was at our house, we all sat at the table and I said: I want to go to Russia. Then you should join the folk dancing troupe, my father said right away, and Luigi laughed out loud. You won't make a dime there, boy, he said, you'll have to bring your own money! And everyone laughed. Only my mother supported me.

Moscow nevertheless remained my goal. The etched glass picture of Russia broke in the earthquake. I still remember it. We went back to the house the next day to have a look around, to see what we could save, and the etched glass picture lay there broken in two, while the window was shattered in a thousand pieces. The small chain attached to the lead frame held the picture together. We can fix this, I said, but my father grew angry, tearing it out of my hand. Later he actually glued it back together and hung it in the window himself, but it must have slipped while he was gluing it, and hairlines moved outwards from the central crack, like streams lining a river on a map, and everything about this landscape of onion domes was crooked. Still. It was nice that it hung in the window again.

BILE MAŠKIRE

At carnival, the most important celebration in the valley, the masqueraded perform. There are *lipe bile maškire*, the beautiful white masks as messengers of spring, and *kukaci maškire*, the ugly winter ancients. The men and women who masquerade in white all wear the same costume: a long white skirt adorned with colourful cording, a white shirt and a colourful belt. On their heads, a prodigious

116

bonnet, bedecked with colourful paper flowers. Some bonnets dangle colourful ribbons that hide one's face; all roaming strangers by no account recognizable, white as the limestone mountains and not-white as the flowers from the interglacial period that managed to salvage themselves, whiling in the cracks of the limestone peak that towered over the glacier.

OLGA

I'm not from the valley. My father is, but I'm not. I grew up in Venezuela. I'm an only child. My mother and grandmother were from Sicily. They were in Venezuela longer than my father. My father and my mother met in Caracas. My father actually wanted to move to the countryside, but ended up staying in the city. They both worked in a shoe factory. We lived in the city outskirts, where almost everyone on our street was Italian, all in small, low houses with yards. Nearly everyone had chickens, and some people even kept a pig. The pigs were smaller there than here, and they had dark bristles. I was startled when I saw my first European pig, it seemed big as a cow. The yards were all compact trampled earth, and even in the kitchen we only had a solid dirt ground, no flooring. It's a gypsy floor, my grandmother always said. The most beautiful thing was a large tree with pink blossoms; when it bloomed it filled the entire house with its scent. My parents went to work, and my grandmother stayed home. Once I started school she would bring me there and pick me up. One day she never came. I waited alone at the gate after all the other children had gone home. Then a neighbour woman came and said: Come on, I'll bring you home, something happened, your grandmother can't pick you up. She gave me a piece of nougat and at that moment

117

I knew it was bad. Why else would she give me sweets? My grandmother had been hit by a car and lay at home in bed, her eyes closed, a bit of blood about her mouth. My mother sat beside her, crying, and I'm not sure whether my grandmother was still alive at that point; the candles were burning already. My mother screamed and cried and slammed her head against the bedposts. My grandmother was buried, and from then on after school a neighbour child and his mother brought me all the way to our street, and from there I walked alone the rest of the way to our small house, where I waited for my parents. My mother was always sad. One morning she had a headache so bad she couldn't get out of bed. When I got home from school she was in the hospital, and the next day she died. Perhaps she died of unhappiness, a neighbour woman suggested. That's when my father decided to move back to Italy. We had no one left in Venezuela.

Shortly after we arrived from Venezuela I joined the Resia choir. I had always liked to sing and still remembered all the songs my mother had taught me. My teacher said right away: You have such a beautiful voice. The music in the valley is something special. At first I found it awful, especially compared to the songs of my mother, but also to the ones from home, from Venezuela, that we had learned in school. Outsiders think our music all sounds the same, but that's not true. It's played on two fiddles and a *bunkula*, which is a type of bass. With their feet the fiddlers stomp the beat while they play. The higher and lower parts of the melody always alternate precisely, like two sides of the same thing, and the players stomp the high melody with their left foot, and the deeper one with their right foot. The fiddlers even wear special shoes when they play, black and buckled. The men play the instruments, the women sing. There are also girls who can

118

play the fiddle, but that's always been somewhat frowned upon. Girls are put on this Earth to sing, an old fiddler once said in front of me. I liked singing in the choir. When I sang I could forget everything: my mother, Venezuela – life, even. The songs were all about the mountains or flowers or love. But the words weren't important. Only the voices were important. The tone. Until you no longer knew which voice in the choir was your own. The melodies were neither sad nor cheerful, but plaintive and yet in a way serene. As if you'd lost something, or something had disappeared or broken and could never be found or made whole again, and you could only sing about it, you couldn't change a thing anyway. I never thought about the mountains the songs were about – I saw them every day, after all. The songs dealt with something I couldn't see. Something that I'd never even had. I think that's why a choir sounds so beautiful: everyone is thinking something different as they sing. Everyone has a different feeling that there are no words for, just this song alone. I especially like the Song of Riba Faronika. While singing it you had to move your hands in front of your chest like a snake: that represented the waves, since Riba Faronika lives in the ocean. We choir girls got along well. There was never any derision or jealousy. Somehow every voice found its place within the entirety. Later I also enjoyed wearing the outfit. It was like becoming a different person. A person who still had a mother and always had lived here. Sometimes we helped each other get dressed, with fastening the scarves and belts. That was also fun. And for carnival we wore giant bonnets with flowers we made ourselves. I have not a single bad memory of singing in the choir. But it still ended suddenly for me. One day I came home from school and didn't want to sing any more. I couldn't explain it to anyone, not even to myself.

119

Sometimes it made me sad to hear the other girls sing, sometimes it didn't move or interest me in the slightest. As if part of me was a musical doll that I'd locked away with a key, which no longer made a sound. There were dolls like that back then, with a string on their backs that you could pull, and little holes in their stomachs, from which their voices came. They never moved their mouths, of course. My aunt gave me a doll like that when we arrived from Venezuela, but at that point I was already too old for dolls. Maybe she wanted one for herself.

Later, after the earthquake, we sung occasionally, when several of us were together. While cooking or doing the dishes outside. We really had lost something, and had every reason for these wistful songs, but actually we sang them to cheer ourselves up, to remember happy times. Of course it was the experience of the earthquake and the horror that followed it which made these remembered times 'happy'. Now, when I can't sleep sometimes I try to remember the songs we sang back then. They're still inside me somewhere, the melodies always come back, but the words come back only in part. My voice in the dark, alone, sounds so small, like a little bird that doesn't know how to sing on its own. It's more of a peep.

THE SAGA OF RIBA FARONIKA

An old story about the origin of the world goes like this:

God separated water and land. Then he took a handful of sand and threw it into the sea. A grain of sand landed on Riba Faronika's back, and she stirred.

Who is Riba Faronika? A mermaid whose fishtail is cleft into two parts. She slept on the ocean floor, and God's grain of sand woke her. If Riba Faronika twitches one of her tails, an earthquake happens on that side of the world. If she turns around in the water, the entire world is inundated by a flood.

Riba Faronika's every movement – yes, even if she twitches in her sleep – delivers calamity across the world. Does she know that? No one can say, because even the vaguest beginning of an answer – even if the mermaid should prick her ears to hear the question – might mean humanity's end.

People sing to Riba Faronika, to keep her gentle and still. In one song Jesus stands on the shore and instead of throwing sand into the sea he summons Riba Faronika to spare humanity.

Riba Faronika gives no answer. The melody describes the movement of the waves.

GIGI

In times past in spring they sent us boys up to the high meadows to scythe, rake together, and carry the grass in a basket to the village. The grass was for our goats. In spring the goats waited for the herbs and flowers that grew up there below the chalk cliffs. For the grass we had panniers: deep, woven baskets that we fastened onto our backs. Pannier weaving was an art form only few mastered. Choosing the right moment to harvest the hazelnut twigs, peeling and soaking and bending. Everything can be an art form. As long as beautiful spring grass grew up there, the scythes waited in a small stone hut. Scything is also an art form. Whetting on the stone and the angle of the blade while cutting. Scything is different in every weather. Occasionally it's as if the blade were alive, and not of steel. The grass smelled something sweet.

Up on the meadows were *stavoli*. Huts for the herders with cows and goats. In times past the people in the valley led two different lives. Their summer lives, up there in the *stavoli* with the livestock, and their winter lives down below in the village. On some mountain pastures there were enough *stavoli* to house an entire village. The people also had fields and gardens up there, and cut hay for winter. Back then, in the time of the earthquake, few people went up there. The paths up the mountain are very steep. Sometimes there would be two, maybe three shepherds who drove a small herd of cows and goats up there, and stayed for the summer. To milk and make cheese. Some were migrant workers not from here. And always a few people liked it and wanted to stay. But no one did stay.

Once during a storm there had been a heavy mudslide and the scree field that we had to cross was strewn with boulders, broken off the cliffs above. Nothing but fresh white limestone. In times past they would have brought them to the limestone kilns, further down in the forest.

We climbed over the boulders and emerged on the hillside high above our meadow. That day our panniers were only half full, since we had lost so much time clambering over the stones, and when we got home we were hit – no one cared how many boulders had lain in our way.

In summer sometimes I spent entire days up in the meadow, alone with the goats. Not by the *stavoli*, where other people were. I went to the meadow where we scythed; I called it my mountain pasture. It was pretty steep, too steep for cows. From there one looked over the entire valley. There were a few villages on small hills, and our brook of a river. The valley looked like a hand that had pushed its way between the mountains, nudging them to the side. The hills with villages were the fingers' knuckles. Everything becomes so strange when so small and seen from a great distance, as if it were suddenly snipped out from your own life. Where could I now be down below,

I wondered. A small dot moving along a path. Nothing more.

MOUNTAIN OF PURGATORY
In Dante's *Divine Comedy*, the mountain of purgatory depicts atonement in the purgatorial fire. The mountain is described as a cone with seven levels, which can be ascended on a spiralling path. The seeking poet and wayfarer, roamer, follows this path and learns, from his encounters with people in the process of purification, that every deliverance into the next world – leading out of the limbo of atonement and into paradise – is accompanied by an earthquake in this world.

IV

'Just as we speak of a submerged Tyrrhenis and seek, by means of zoo-geographical and phyto-geographical studies, to discover the relationship and connexion between such of its remaining fragments as rise above the level of the sea, so we may likewise speak of an Adriatis submerged in later times, and endeavour to determine its outline... All these great lines, from Montenegro to Lake Idro, bound the Adriatic Sea on the east, north, and north-west, and may be appropriately termed the peri-Adriatic fractures.'
—— Eduard Suess, *The Face of the Earth*, vol. 1 (1892)

PATH OF THE DOG

The path is named after a sad incident. One day a hiker died while climbing Canin. He arrived in the village one day in May, early in the morning. He had a dog with him: 'my loyal friend', he called it. The hiker drank a coffee at the bar and purchased a few provisions from the grocery next door. He was humorous and in good spirits, and he told the few people standing around in the bar, as well as the woman at the cash register, that he wanted to climb Canin. Bravo, said the men, good luck! The woman at the cash register told him about the terrible storms of a few weeks prior, about the unseasonable spring thunder that buffeted the mountains, making everything tremble, bringing back the old fear of the earthquake. She had pulled her children out of bed and placed them below a doorframe, and further down in the valley it was inundated with water as to set scree falling, unleashing such a dark rumble, too, but it never turned into an avalanche.

Thankfully, the hiker said. Outside he exchanged a few words with the cook, who stood in the sun smoking. Then he left.

He seemed to know his way around. Later a few people said they thought they had already seen him a few times. Someone even suggested he was a regular. But who can really say, in retrospect – after all, hikers look alike, in colourful clothing that shields against the wind and weather, some with dogs, others without, some with poles, others without. In any event, this hiker with a dog walked up the steps between the houses and then past the gardens in the rear village. Along a garden fence he allegedly stopped and talked to someone about the local garlic, the small white garlic of the region.

Behind the village the hiker climbed downhill and then turned left, entering a damp, shadowy basin, and then hung upslope again, following the rushing sound of the wild brook flowing below, and from above from one spot it looks like a real river, frothing green around the large stones, bordered by forested hillsides, and there's nothing to hear but this rushing, and so it remains for a while, through open forests, all the way to a bridge over the brook that comes rushing down from Monte Sart, from which it gets its name. Near the bridge the two brooks join, forming a rivulet. The bridge is made of wood; deep down the small quick streams roil and the shadows of fish flicker in the still, roiling pools between boulders. On the other shore the path leads steeply uphill, over stone steps and secured wooden ones, up the open slope into the forest. The beautiful beech forest. The light falls in pale, steamy strips between the trunks onto the old foliage on the ground. Downhill: beeches, uphill: strips of spruces, pines, firs. Bells ring, axes sound, chainsaws howl, but all the same, any sense of direction is lost, and everything that sounds and rings and drones might just as well be a memory, a memento of sound, from other beech forests, from other times and places – nothing but tones from somewhere, tones from sometime, not ascribable to any visible thing. On the wayside heather grows in thick cushions, on the spruce-and-pine side of the path blueberry bushes grow. On the beech-side of the northward escarpments are the heart-shaped leaves of cyclamen, violets, wrinkled leaves of primrose close to the soil. Occasionally the trees thin, offering a vista across further forests in the whitish light of day. The path is very narrow, two people would not be able to walk side by side – hard to believe livestock was driven to the mountain pastures here, cows and goats and sheep. Closer to the water, in the hollows of the forest are limestone kilns, where in former times white pieces of limestone from the streams were tossed. White limestone

127

from the upper valley and black bitumen from the lower one – that's how the people earned their bread.

The dog would have rummaged about; whistled back to the limestone kilns, with their overgrown hollows, the dog follows the command, panting.

Did the hiker occasionally have a sense of trepidation? Did he take breaks? For a while the way leads through the forest with little incline, then it goes slightly downhill, back to the water, where the valley widens, overgrown with low brushwood. Ferns on the wayside. Green alders. The path climbs again to the east, where it is more open, steep, edged by bell flowers; the forest becomes sparser. A karstic mountain pasture takes over from the forest. Small chalky ridges bulge out between patches of short, scrubby grass, widow flowers bloom all summer long, knapweeds, yarrow, cranesbill, clover. Further up is a small building for livestock, hay and shepherds, a refuge, a shelter in former times. Today there is only a single token hut, a 'since-the-year-dot' piece, selected from among a few ruins to be built up again. Livestock have not grazed on the pasture for a long time, at most a herd of sheep, brought over by transhumance herders from the other side of the border. Occasionally they scythe here, drying the hay on the racks.

From the alpine pasture the gaze is met directly by the ridge's greenly veined lower rock slopes, from the Sart peak to Canin. One can make out trails, stone stairways. The violence responsible for the massif's creation is inscribed into the slanting layers of rock along the ridge, and yet at the same time the path, appearing as if outlined against the rock, looks so mild, so nonviolent and inviting, in twists and incremental rises, with cliffs arching over depressions as if to shield them; a rigid feeling of security is painted in the mind of the beholder, a

128

trust in this formation of stone, which after an extended period of time watching the valley at its feet – its coming-into-being, its troubles and its tremors – is perhaps well disposed to it, after all. To the peak! the hiker must have thought, with the fierce ambition of a mountain climber who is not satisfied by the sight of it alone – sheltered from wind, solid ground beneath their feet – but wants to see what the mountain sees, this valley streaked white by watercourses and dappled by infrequent settlements on hillsides, jammed between mountain ridges. In the white light of an overcast day, the terrain lies without shadow. Everything appears so smoothed and lucid. A mountain can be read differently in every light, searched differently for traces. A scree fall that might have buried beneath it who knows whom might appear soft and nestled into an oblong depression between two slopes, or in a sharp light glisten, as if adorned by white shards. The hiker definitely climbed higher, among stunted trees and lashed alpine roses, across the border of upright bushes, beyond, into the terrain of lichens and stones, followed by his dog; maybe the dog was nervous, anxious, full of foreboding, helpless, the hiker either didn't notice or paid it no mind. Did he take a break, already on the bare stone terrain? Observe the clouds gathering on the peak? Maybe he remembered the saga of the valley, about the clouds searching for their pasture on Canin. The white, grey, greenish, bluish limestone – a mountain pasture for clouds, that's how the story goes, a place where the clouds can eat their fill of white.

The hiker was later found in a hollow full of scree, a gentle basin with a cliff hanging over it. In hindsight people said they had heard snippets of the dog's distant howls for days and taken them for the temper of the wind, for a wile of this or that witch, for a premonition. The poor dog, people said in hindsight, That poor animal, for days. It could hardly stand up, how it ran behind the stretcher, to the helicopter. The path is thus named after a sad incident, perhaps also in warning to the mountain enthusiasts who let themselves be fooled by the colour and inviting incline of the cliffs above the tree line.

LINA

When the earthquake hit, my wedding lay ahead. I still had a proper trousseau with things I had sewn and embroidered. We had bought the fabric in Udine, the only real city that I knew. My fiancé was working in Switzerland, he was supposed to come home in summer. Just for the wedding. What a strange wedding it would be, with all the broken things around, and all the misery. How good that nothing happened to your trousseau, my mother said while straightening up. Our house was relatively unscathed, my bedroom being hit the worst. At some point they said that the houses on the hillside were spared because they were already doled a misfortune. Those houses had been built after a great flood and a landslide carried away the entire lower village. That was a very long time ago, before all of our time, centuries ago, I think; there is nothing left of the former lower village. At any rate, there were no major damages to our house. The ceiling in my room was cracked. Dust, mortar, shards, fallen things – we had all that. The chicken coop slightly crooked. In other places it was much worse, but our village generally made out well. Other villages collapsed entirely, there was nothing left. Today the village across the valley is still just a development of small, low houses, all in a row. First they lived in a tent city, then in emergency housing, small boxes. Eventually the government built them prefab houses that look exactly like the emergency housing.

Then came the wedding, in summer. The earthquake was maybe two months behind us. None of the collapsed things had been rebuilt, people helped one another renovating and rebuilding and in their gardens, too. After all, everyone had to eat. Our church was still standing, but everything took place outside. It was a hot day. I was twenty-five and I thought: Now I've hit this milestone, too. Ours was the first wedding here in the valley after the earthquake, and a newspaper reporter even came and took photographs, and we were in the news, I think even in Udine. It really was a beautiful photograph, even if it looked a bit strange, the short dress with the veil. We hadn't bought the wedding dress yet, and my mother decided that a veil was enough, since it wasn't a time for pomp. My sisters made me the veil, with a crown. I think someone had given them a piece of curtain, but it was a beautiful veil, with small fabric flowers sewn on and a few real blossoms. We all ate outside, the entire village came, as well as people from my husband's village; the wedding was something beautiful for a change, in a time of hardship. We even danced, musicians had come and everyone was happy for the change of pace. It was a real wedding, even if I didn't have a white dress. Later there was a thunderstorm. That's good luck, that's good luck! a few people cried, but then everyone became afraid again once thunder rumbled. This sound never ceases to inspire fear, it still happens to me today. As for the luck that thunder is supposed to bring – I can't say I've noticed any of that, either.

My husband is from a different village in the valley; his parents' house, where we should have moved in, was wrecked. Everyone worked to build it back up again,

131

years passed before we had our own home. But he was gone a lot of the time, and I was happy to remain with my family. Our new lives began, in other words, not with the wedding, but with the earthquake. It changed everything here in the valley.

DANCE

The people in the valley dance like nowhere else in the world. The men and women have different steps for the fiddle and bass music, which is an endless, hardly appreciable variation of a sequence of three or four tones. The men's movements lead in a circle; the women's movements describe a straight line, side to side, back and forth. They never touch. They dance like this for hours, in round figures and angular ones, to the music that seems to repeat only to the unpractised ear accustomed to sweeping melodies; in reality it is always putting forward small new variances. In their lines and circles the dancers always pass one another by, nearly missing each other, intentionally, from ever new angles and directions, and from above they must look like lightless stars, moving their bodies to a spherical music comprehensible only to them, and only in this not-touching, this not-meeting, only by sticking to a distance at times scarcely perceptible – under a constant drawing near and then diverging – do they achieve a great and unfamiliar balance.

ANSELMO

We had a few weeks of school to go, all different grades together outside, when the weather was nice. When it rained we were in the tent, where it was muggy and loud. We were all given brand-new pens and notebooks and drawing pads, and books, too, but there were no real lessons any more. Before summer vacation we talked about what we wanted to become. Someone from the vocational college came and talked to us about various professions, bricklayer and carpenter and electrician. We'll need you soon! he said. Just be good and finish school, and then you can help rebuild our home! At the time I still had three years of school to go and I didn't believe him that it would take so long. Afterwards they asked all the children what they wanted to become, and most of the boys said they wanted to go to Germany. I said I wanted to be a policeman, just because – anything but a bricklayer. And in the end that's exactly what I became. A bricklayer and a tile man. I've done it all. Even marble work. Becoming a policeman was my father's idea, anyway. If you entered the police force you didn't have to do military service.

That summer was nice, actually, at least the beginning, when we could do whatever we wanted outside. Later many children were sent to relatives, outside the valley, in very distant regions. I would have liked to go back to Germany, but my mother never came for us. Once my sister and I wrote her, to say how poorly we were doing: in summer a postal delivery man came on a moped to the village, and he also picked up letters. You could already hear him clattering from far away. We even had money for the stamps. But my mother never answered. Maybe the letter never even arrived, everyone was always complaining about the postal service.

Once a guy from the newspaper came. He reported on our valley and asked various people how they were doing, and photographed them. He herded us children together: we should position ourselves on the meadow so you couldn't see the tents, and smile cheerfully; he asked a few of us our names, and what we wanted to be when we

133

grew up. He never got to me. Later someone brought my father the newspaper with the photograph, he even saved the page, I found it a few years ago in one of his drawers. The children appear cheerful and carefree. They all want to be diligent and help rebuild their home, the caption says. We really do all look cheerful in the photograph, but then again he told us to laugh. The rubble is nowhere to be seen.

Later we children actually did have to help. I had to knock the mortar out of the bricks that had broken loose. My father worked like an animal. Whenever he walked past me, he hit me on the back of my neck, because I wasn't working fast enough. My sister accompanied my grandmother to the field, weeding and watering, harvesting; every day there was a spat. Once we were both supposed to accompany my grandmother to the cemetery, to visit my grandfather's grave. Many stones had fallen down or stood askew, some were broken. It all looked ravaged still, people first had so much work to do on their houses. The stone with the picture of my grandfather stood only slightly askew, not a lot had happened to that row. I never met him; in the gravestone photograph he looked exactly like my father. My sister was still angry, from working in the field. She was supposed to clear away an old bouquet – that didn't suit her and she kicked the gravestone so hard it nearly fell over. May the ground open up and devour you! my grandmother wailed, and then I saw my sister cry for the first time. She was usually such a tough one, like wood, like stone.

Sometimes early in the morning I would follow the goat shepherd, Goat Gigi, just so I didn't have to help on the house. Gigi brought the goats from the village to the meadow, far up; from there one had a view across the entire valley. I was always on the lookout for vipers and practised catching them. I didn't always grab them; I also practised behaving such that they didn't notice me, and I observed precisely the way that they moved, what direction they thrust their heads in. Once I nearly saved Gigi, when he hadn't seen a viper lying on a boulder that he wanted to lean against. That was lucky. Otherwise he doesn't talk, or he only talks to himself and the goats; my father always said he wasn't quite right in the head. But on that day with the viper he showed me a few things, the trails that the bootleggers took, up over Canin's ridge – Yugoslavia was just on the other side. There was a fresh scree avalanche, you could see it clearly, and he also showed me the wreckage of the valley's rearmost village; all the people were shuttled off after the earthquake. And he showed me every brook and every river in the valley that could only be seen from above. After that I thought I wanted to become a shepherd, more than anything else. The next time Gigi was very silent again, or rather he talked only to his goats. I told him about Germany, about my mother and the gravel quarry and about how in Germany there were days when the entire class went out hiking. He always just nodded. But I still preferred going with him, even if it meant I had to take a few slaps afterwards at home. But the part about the vipers put my father back in a good mood, he thought that was brave.

SISMA

The greatest earthquake in the region's history lay more than 600 years in the past. All the cities and villages were in ruins at that time. Thousands died. Rivers changed their course, fissures gaped in the earth where people once walked, drove, marched. We know nothing of the great displacements and shifts, the terrain-changing interference in the sparsely settled valleys. Since then, not a year has gone by without mild quakes, without tremors, without warning shocks beneath the surface. Until 6 May 1976 the *sisma* was a lesson of the ground, associated with beliefs and superstitions, sayings and customs, those pertaining to the devil and the calamities in the mine or while cutting timber, the fires, the floods. Despite hundreds of small seismic shocks and tremors over the course of centuries, no *earthquake* was inscribed into memory, at most it was an event to be held at a distance by magic. The houses were tall and narrow, with the customary narrow wooden passageways outside into the upper floors: entrances to the ventilated attics. The stately buildings imitated the Venetian style, but invoked, in their imitative ornamentation, older, foreign architectures with peculiarities for which a name exists only in the local language. Nothing about these structures could have withstood an earthquake.

The seismic shocks of May divided life and the landscape into a before and after. The before was the object of memory, stories unceasingly layered and blown over by words. One argued over the form of the cliffs, the course of the brooks, the trees that avalanches rolled over. About the whereabouts of objects, the order of things in the house, the fate of animals. Each of these arguments was an attempt at orientation, at carving a path through the rubble of masonry, mortar, split beams and shattered dishes, to understand the world anew. To begin living in a place anew. With one's memories.

MARA
The earthquake brought bad weather. My God, how it rained. And it turned cold. Later it even snowed. And

the ground trembled again and again. It delivered a shock every time, but I stopped being scared before long. Plaster fell down, things rattled and clattered and fell over, but that was it. I wanted to stay in the house, where my mother was totally calm. She sat in bed, combing grit from her hair. But then the soldiers arrived and set up tents, and a few of them went from house to house, assessing the damages they said, and decided which houses were un-inhabitable. Ours was one of them. We were supposed to move into a tent as well. That was bad. My mother struggled with her hands and feet. By then she spoke only our language, which the soldiers didn't understand, but I took her hand and we walked behind them, and they al-lotted us a spot in a tent. My mother was very silent. She let it all out down below, so to speak, and both our tent neighbours complained. Take your mother home, they said, Take her back. For sure, nothing will happen. Then they were allowed to relocate, because it stank. So we had more room. Everyone argued. But people also told a lot of stories. Someone said that in another village, on the oth-er side of the valley, a paralyzed woman was so startled by the first impact of the earthquake that she jumped up, suddenly able to walk, and made it all the way to the riv-er, where she fell into the water and drowned. I imagined what would happen if my mother went to the river. But she only tried to go home a few times, and after that just sat in the corner. It was difficult to wash her, as she no longer wanted to stand up for anything. After a week or so, I took her back to the house. I started straightening up. That at least gave me something to do. Time passed slowly. Occasionally the neighbours came and helped a bit; they brought a young tree trunk to hold up the ceiling in one room, that was a big help.

The aftershocks continued for days. Occasionally

something in the house toppled, mortar and plaster fell frequently from the ceiling. Everything tasted like dust. I stopped checking on the crack in the rear wall. There was shocking news constantly. How many dead. How much wreckage. What happened in other villages in the valley: those missing, injured, gone mad. My knife-grinder brother returned. He talked about the state of things outside, Venzone covered in rubble and ashes. I remembered the oriole, how my father had imitated it. In the forest behind Venzone, he said back then. Do the birds stay when something like this happens? There seemed to be fewer birds around us after the earthquake. It was also quieter in the forest. Depending on where you were, you didn't hear the noise from the village. Then you could pretend everything was normal again. I also returned to the field. Life had to go on, you know. Everything continued to grow, despite the earthquake. The beans, the cabbage, the potatoes. Everything.

That summer little time was left for the forest, but I managed to go once or twice while my brother was home, taking the steep path towards Monte Sart. In the forest I was calm – the earthquake was barely visible there, aside from a few fallen trees, that was it. And the collapsed *stavoli* on the upper open meadows. It was so silent, with not a single cow grazing on the high meadows, not a shepherd, and so few birds singing. Once I saw a man, walking straight across the forest; I didn't know him. That put me in a state of shock. I was never afraid in the forest until that day. I remembered what we went through with the lunatic from Bologna. A lunatic had escaped the asylum, bringing along a lot of money. The police came, together with the Alpini, asking if anyone in the valley had seen him. He was said to be small and lean, and very quick. And dangerous, they said. A dangerous lunatic from the

138

asylum in Bologna. Suddenly everyone saw the lunatic somewhere. Behind their shed, in the forest, up by the *stavoli*. A few of the sightings were confirmed by the police afterwards. The women were afraid to be home alone, the children were not supposed to play outside. Like a cloud, talk about the lunatic loomed over everything. Where did he get his money? What did he want from us in the valley? Everyone speculated about the lunatic. And then they caught him. High up on the slope beneath Canin, one night he lit a fire, near the mountaineer shelter. The blaze was so great it was visible below in the valley, and someone informed the police, who came and climbed up there with a few Alpini. They had flashlights and for a while from below one could make out little dots, moving through the dark. But the lunatic was unaware, certainly already asleep when they arrived. In any case, they caught him, and led him in handcuffs through the village. He really was a small man, eyes ablaze, black and blazing like glowing coals, and he looked at me as they led him past. Supposedly he wanted to flee to Yugoslavia, over Canin. Yugoslavia is right on the other side. He had to relinquish the money. People around here talked about the lunatic from Bologna for months. Where his money came from, how he made it here on foot from Bologna, that they were waiting for him over there in Yugoslavia, that he was dangerous, although no one could say why. He hadn't touched anyone or anything around here. Not even a chicken went missing. The stranger walked quickly downhill through the forest without looking around, maybe he didn't even notice me. And it couldn't have been a runaway lunatic; the asylums around here had already shut their doors. There were no longer any asylums proper, with barred windows and the like. So no one could escape.

PARTISANS

The old women say it happened like this:

The partisans came from two sides. Who would we stand by? Both sides were against the fascists, but also against each other. Would we stand by the Italians? Would we stand by the Slovenians? We stood by our children and goats and pigs and chickens. The Slovenians showed up at our door at night, threatening to kill us if we didn't give them our pigs. You're our brothers and sisters, they said from behind their guns. The pigs squealed in the darkness, they sounded twice as loud as they did by day. Would they have preferred going to the Italians? They certainly were not afraid. Pigs are curious creatures. Even on the way to slaughter they are pert and they look around as if the whole wide world were just waiting for them. Later one heard them screaming all night, this shrill screeching when it was a matter of their lives, from such a distance it sounded eerie and gruesome.

Then the Italians came for the chickens. The white cheese. The bacon. The woody pears. They too came in the night. Slender boys and girls. First they asked for the pig. The pig had already been taken. Sometimes they forced their way in through the kitchen, into the yard, to check whether the stall was really empty. They weren't accustomed to the sheds beneath the kitchen. You're standing by the Slovenians? was always the next question. Hand over your chickens. They had sacks, like the Slovenians. Tell us, who do you stand by? these anxious children asked, bleary-eyed at the door. Hey, who's it going to be? We're fighting for you. The children looked on, wide-eyed. They all wanted to fight. We were probably all more on the Italians' side. Nothing but the garlic did they leave us, the heads so small they went unnoticed, this sweet garlic that only grows around here. The goats

140

they also spared us. Goats are difficult animals, they die ornery, perfidious.

TONI

Later that summer workers came from Yugoslavia, to help with the clean-up. Slovenians, mostly. Their language is a little bit like ours, and they spoke no Italian. Of course, you're our brothers, they said. They also had damages at home from the earthquake, but not as bad as around us. They pitched in with everything. One of them always let me help out, even allowed me to ride with him in the truck. Where should all this rubble go, he always said. You could build an entire mountain out of it. I was allowed to stand in the bed and they handed me the lighter things. Most people tried to save material: bricks that weren't broken, window frames and wooden beams and roof shingles. There was no new building material yet, but everyone wanted to fix up their houses. Around us people threw nothing away, they saved everything. Some people had a yard full of wood and old roof shingles, all neatly stacked and bundled. Grey from the sun and frost, or covered in moss where it stood in the shadows. Just don't throw it out. The earthquake taught us all a lesson there. Everything can become useless in an instant. Later, when there was money, some people abandoned their patched-up houses and built something brand new in front of the village, even buildings with multiple apartments, just like in the city. But that was later, and by then I was already gone.

Around us, most houses and the church were still standing, and our bells rang, too. Once I went with the men to the neighbouring village, where nearly every house had collapsed. They had brought along little prefab houses from Yugoslavia that could be built up quickly; they looked like animal sheds and were erected on a meadow outside the village. And inside the village things were strewn every which way: tiles, the large stones old houses were built from, the balconies, roof trusses, furniture, sinks.

I don't know where they brought all the debris. Later I heard they dumped it outside the valley in the big river. I don't know if that's true. Around us, too, some things were thrown in the river, and in steeply descending gorges; they just tilted the bed of the truck and all the debris came crashing down, sounding like an avalanche. Once the entire truck nearly skidded down, because the driver reversed too far. But everything worked out. And what should they have done, with all those stones and remains. Stone to stone, they said as they dumped the debris into a gorge. I had fun driving around with them and helping. Come to us in Yugoslavia, they said, you're a valiant worker, and you can practically speak our language. I'd rather go to the Russians, I told the one guy, and he laughed and laughed.

In the evenings the Yugoslavians liked to build a fire and sing, and some of the songs were familiar to me, the one about Riba Faronika, for one. Around here it's the women who sing that song. One of the Yugoslavians told me they had mountains just like ours, but they were in the sea. White cliff islands. I had never been to the seaside and wasn't sure if it was true. I couldn't imagine it at all. He promised to send me a postcard with a picture of the mountains in the sea, but it never arrived. He was right, though – I saw it later when I was there, by the sea, in Croatia. After the war. The islands lay white and bare in the ocean like mountain ridges that had slipped off.

It was a strange summer. All that confusion. And so

many misfortunes, one after the other – accidents and thunderstorms, and it just didn't stop. I worked with the Yugoslavians for about two weeks. Then they left. I no longer wanted to work with the debris myself. After that I helped my father with the house; he wasn't working, as the factory had also been destroyed. But the factories were reconstructed before anything else – a lot of people were angry about it, but later everyone was proud. Later everything was different, when people looked back on the earthquake summer. That summer I thought I never wanted to work construction. But then I became a bricklayer, after all; I went to the vocational college, as did my cousin. I didn't like studying. Once we had finished our studies it was time for military service. Everyone was drafted, except for me, by mistake. So I went to Russia. To Moscow. Building high-rises. We were a whole group of Italians, and twice a year we were allowed to fly home. We made good money and had good accommodation. I quickly learned Russian, but the others had a hard time. Some never learned it. I liked being there – those were my happiest years. When I returned to the valley to visit, I was only a guest. At weddings and family gatherings they always said: Come on, sing something in Russian. Unfortunately, I could – a good many songs, and I knew them better than those from the valley. And when I was home, something was missing. The streets that never ended. The massive construction sites. The foreign people brushing past me. Thousands. Every day. But then I left, after all. Today I am sorry I did. I would have been better off staying.

MARA

Once we were back in the house I started tidying up. Not only the kitchen and my room, but also the small rooms where I had not set foot for a long time. Everything was covered in years' worth of dust and spiderwebs, but I also saw small earthquake damages, areas where large blots of plaster had fallen off, a broken window unnoticed until then. A mirror had slipped from its nail and cracked down the middle. That was in the room where a chest of my old clothing stood. I hadn't opened it for a long time. Everything felt dirty. Dust, moisture, a musty smell. I looked at my old dresses – the few that I had, which I wouldn't have been able to wear any more. I too was once young, I thought, although I wasn't even that old yet. In the chest I also found the carnival bonnet I'd once made for myself, the year I went masqueraded in white, as a messenger of spring beneath a large flower bonnet. We girls made all the flowers by hand – it was a fun winter, and I thought: Maybe I'll fall in love this carnival. I made myself a bonnet with colourful ribbons that hung in front of my face, to hide behind. My clothes didn't give away my identity, either, since no one wears these white dresses on any other occasion, and everyone had the same stockings and shoes. I danced a lot that carnival, and even my own brother didn't recognize me. After all those years the bonnet smelled rank, and the paper flowers were very limp, some having even fallen off, but I still put it on and looked at myself in the mirror – the cracked one – crouching down a bit, since it was on the floor. I saw myself between the ribbons covering my face, and did not recognize myself. Never would I go out like that again, and perhaps there would never even be another carnival in our valley of rubble.

NUNATAK

A nunatak is a summit or a mountain that protrudes from late Pleistocene glacial ice, of which it itself is free. The ridges and peaks that edge the valley in the east and northeast were once peaks and spurs of this kind, towering over the shimmering glaciers of the ice age. Rugged and fragmented, they project above rock polished by the glacial ice as it slipped downward, and throughout the glacial period they gave shelter, in their cracks and cliffs, to seeds and plants, which in the warm interims have since reoccupied the land. Developed from life forms, zoophytes, radiata and molluscs that had compressed into limestone, the grooved, layered, fissured rock offered a refuge where saxifrage, hen-and-chicks, and winter heath survived, in order to – after the affront of ice and frost and the glacier's retreat – wander back towards the valley.

LINA

Did it storm often that summer? I can't remember. Whoever was able tilled their field, the corn grew, so did the beans. I remember one storm that followed a very hot day, the sky appearing as yellow to me as it had on the day of the earthquake. But by evening the sky over Canin was already so dark blue, a sullen blue, and just after it turned dark it began to thunder. Lightning bolts struck right away, too, as rarely happens, and a wind howled and drummed on the shutters, and then it began to hail such that you couldn't hear your own voice for the pelting, and no one rang the bells. Before, when it thundered someone always stood ready to ring the bells – said to keep hail at bay – but now it was as if it didn't matter. There were few tents left around us, quite a few people had already put their houses back in order, others had gone to their relatives, above all those with young children. I felt sorry for the people in the tents, and the next day one could see what the gales of wind and hail and rain had served.

My husband left shortly after the wedding, despite initially bragging about the bonus vacation days they gave him in Switzerland, because of the wedding and the earthquake. But I think he was done with toiling. Because he came from outside and at the same time was from here, everyone asked for his help at home, but also in his village, where things were in a bad state. Grab a hold of this, do that, every day it was the same, above all at his parents'. So he left. A few weeks later he sent money collected by his colleagues, for the earthquake victims. Swiss francs. I put it in a drawer – what should I have done? – first it had to be exchanged. And I didn't trust my brother with it.

Once I went to Udine with someone from the village. Luigi, the guy with the German children. I had heard he was driving into town. The children sat in the backseat of the car, hitting one another and bickering, but in German, so I didn't understand. They need new shoes, Luigi said, school is starting again soon. It was nice to walk around the city. The bank took a long time, the man looked at me as if I'd stolen the money. But I knew what to expect with the currency exchange. My husband sent it to us from Switzerland, for the earthquake victims, I explained. Afterwards I ate an ice cream and looked at window displays. Luigi was already waiting with his kids. We stopped in Gemona to look at the destruction, it was awful. Some people were living in destroyed houses, without a roof over their heads, behind a curtain of blankets and tarps. I kept a few bills and gave the rest of the money to our mayor. Who knows what he did with it.

FORMATION OF THE MOUNTAINS:
FIRST BELIEF

At the centre of Earth is a fire that melts all material, expelling it through thinner areas of the Earth's crust. Mountains and rises form wherever the crust encompassing this unrelenting, burning heat is not yet stable enough to resist the blaze. The momentum of the expulsion determines the height of the mountains, and the speed at which the fiery, molten material solidifies determines their shape. A theory, a belief that banks on the vulnerability, the inevitable raw spot in the Earth's shell, in the skin, the fortification. Every mountain is thus an ejection, obtained by an exploitation of that vulnerability, beneath which it continued to burn; every ridge a moment of horror, the irrevocable entrance into a different state; every peak is a testimony to being at the mercy of the power balance between element and material.

GIGI

On the evening of the earthquake I left the village. Through the rain and wind and thunder, I took the goats up to my mountain pasture. What was I thinking? I don't know any more. In any case, I couldn't handle being in the village, with all the commotion. I felt as I had in the mental hospital, way back. That was forever ago, but it lay inside me somewhere and was awoken. The screams and the fear – you can't see it but it's there, and it grabs you by the throat, these kicks and thumps and the hard hands of the guards, how they yelled over my shoulder into my ear: Want to go to the locked ward, do you? Want to go to the locked ward? No one wanted to go to the locked ward, to the restless, where they lay around at sixes and sevens – naked, it was said, men and women – and they bit and struck and kicked and bred, without a door or a window you could open from inside. But that's just what I heard; I was never in there. And before long I was released and went home and never returned, and it wasn't until the earthquake that it all came back to me. In any case, I left the village, and when I was in the forest I feared more for the goats than myself; in the dark, everything was so foreign and unreliable, and at one point we had to climb over a landslide that had taken down trees along with it, and on the other side I no longer knew if we were going the right way – it was dark, everything so different than in the bright light of day, but I think the goats knew where we were, because they just went on ahead, two whitish shadows. The way seemed so long to me, so long, as if we walked all night, yet it was still a deep black once we arrived at the pasture, and the huts were still standing, solid and straight. Let's just hope no one else gets the idea, I thought.

Below in the valley I saw a fire. It couldn't have been our village, as it is not at all visible from above. It was the village across the river, where my sister lived. Later we found out that the village was destroyed almost entirely. My sister's house included. But then, on that evening, I didn't think about my family at all. I was just happy to be up there. Today I would say I had no thoughts at all.

I stayed up there in my mountain pasture until the tremors stopped. I can't remember for how many days. Maybe a week, maybe longer. No one came that entire time. It was cold, rain fell, once it even snowed. I made a fire, I milked the goats, I picked herbs – everything I could find that was edible. I hardly moved. I lay there and sat and watched the valley when the clouds weren't hanging too low, and I always waited for the tremors. Every day. I listened for the air, and heard birds: birds of prey, jackdaws. The first corncrake. It called at night, *krek krek*. Infrequently, as if merely trying something out. It must have just arrived from Africa, or who knows where. Sensed nothing of the earthquake. What's an earthquake to the birds? *Scythe grinder* is what we call the corncrake here.

Sometimes I also heard a muffled thunder, neither the weather nor the quake; it came from the mountains, boulders that broke loose, or the deep abysses in the limestone when they collapsed. I never strayed far from the goats. It was different than usual in the pasture, because I knew something bad had happened below, and because I didn't know what would be waiting for me when I returned.

I'd never spent so many days alone in the pasture. Sometimes I just said words to myself. Bed. Plate. Stairs. Jacket. Pot. What is a word like that, when the thing isn't there? Would you forget it, if you didn't say it for a long time? These days have remained a hole in my life, of sorts. A hole that I could peer through onto something else, into an unfamiliar world. But that was something positive.

Soon as the quakes were good and over I went back down to the valley. With the goats. I hadn't yet seen in the light of day what had happened. That was a shock. Broken roofs, cracked walls, collapsed building extensions and entire houses yawning. My father got to work on our house; he was a trained bricklayer, he knew what he was doing. Once he saw me he picked up a stone as if to throw it at me, but in the end he didn't, after all. The barn looked even worse than I had imagined. I got to work right away without saying a word. The goats just stood there. By evening I had built a shelter for them. Our house was inhabitable again. There was food at the tents. I felt bad for the people in the tents. A young woman stood in front

of me in line for food, crying. I took a seat at the very end
of a table, and it was all like a bad dream. What had this
one night done to us? My mother came and slapped me
hard on the back of my neck, as she used to do, when I
was young and caused trouble. But after that, everything
was fine. My father didn't say a word to me all summer.

MUSIC

Bagpipes have died out in the valley. But once, outfit-
ted with two or three drones, it was the most important
instrument here. Today the valley's instruments are the
fiddle and a three-stringed bass with two strings of metal
and one of gut, and when they really come together and
ring as one, from a distance it sounds like bagpipes. The
feet of the fiddlers, too, are an instrument: they wear black
buckled shoes and stomp tirelessly to the beat. How to
describe the music? It is neither sad nor happy, in its mi-
nor variations it is infinite, grinding and rasping against
life, with its rhythm that never changes and its small
modifications to the melody. There are words, but only
a few, and they seem unimportant. What's important is
that the music does not stop, the feet continue stomping,
too, keeping the spirits at bay, and the fiddle melody and
the bass that supports it and drives it on – it, too, always
has to keep going, and the dancing cannot stop, those
small variations in the steps and circles, always a drill for
infinitude.

OLGA

Before the earthquake I took the bus to Gemona every
morning. The trip lasted nearly an hour including all
the stops, but that didn't bother me. In the morning I

was still tired. I looked out the window and let my mind wander. And when we reached the expanse where the Tagliamento exits the Carnic Alps and the land comes undone, I always felt so happy, it became open and bright and I always thought, now I'm almost at the sea. I imagined the sea very close and then I was awake. I worked at an office in Gemona, for a dispatch business. I had always wanted to study, and then I went to a commercial college and trained to be a secretary. Typing and shorthand and writing invoices and such. There was a driver I liked. He always came into the office and waited for me to finish filling out his delivery note. Once he invited me to the cinema. After work I changed my clothes and put on make-up in the office bathroom. But I didn't like the film. It was creepy. Afterwards we went for an ice cream. The man drank a beer. I can't even remember his name any more. I'll give you a ride home, he offered, he had a moped. But then he realized how far it was. He kept turning around and calling back to me: Are we almost there? I felt uncomfortable, and so when we reached the fork in the road down below, I said, This is where I live. I think he was afraid he wouldn't have enough petrol to make it home. I walked up through the forest. My aunt was angry at me. She had sat up waiting, but fell asleep in her chair, holding the little hand broom – maybe she wanted to hit me. The girls in the office all laughed the next morning. Why didn't you stroll with him all night? they asked. Why didn't you go up to the castle? Now that would've been romantic! What should I have said? I felt a bit embarrassed in the presence of the driver and avoided him, and whenever he stood around with the other drivers in the yard and they laughed I thought, now they're laughing about me. Yes, in the morning I was happy to drive out of the valley, but in the evening I was happy to go back home. Although a small sadness always welled up in me, whenever the mountains closed behind me. As if I was afraid I were seeing them for the last time. Humans are a peculiar kind. They always think about what's missing. When you're in the mountains, you miss the expanse, when you're in the plains, you miss the mountains. It's all about what isn't there. I wonder if that's how it is for animals. For birds, for example. In summer, when they sit on their eggs and sing, are they thinking about their journeys and the part of Africa where they live in winter? When they're there in Africa, do they think about our mountains, our valley? Our forest? Is it even the same birds that return, or is it always different ones? Who can say.

I can't remember exactly when the soldiers arrived. Was it on the third day, or the fourth? The roads and lanes were buried in rock and avalanche debris. No one came, no one left. Arriving along with the soldiers were people from the civil defence and the fire department, some coming from very far away, Como and Brescia and Livorno. They told us about what happened outside. Gemona completely destroyed. Quit your moaning, they said, you've got it good here. Many people had died in Gemona. That was worse for me than what had happened to us. Of course you think about other people. What about my colleagues? But I also thought about my job. About how it was all over now. The office, the bus ride. I was saving up for a Vespa. Nothing would be the same.

When I went to the commercial college in Gemona, sometimes I would get off the bus early, already at the fork in the road, and go the rest of the way by foot. Often through the forest, cutting straight across; it was steep, but I liked walking among the beeches. I just had to be careful with my shoes. Once something bad happened to me. I saw a hanged man in a tree. I saw between the branches the feet, the brown shoes. I looked up, but didn't see his face. I was startled already when I saw the legs, the body. I ran off in my fright, straight down the hill, and then I had to climb back up over stone and rock, and then back down; when I arrived home, immediately, the question: Where were you? I missed the bus, I said, hiding my shoes behind my back, because they were completely scuffed and grey from the boulders and stones. I secretly cleaned them up, but they were no longer nice. I couldn't eat a thing, I just sat at the table. And I didn't say anything about the man in the tree, because suddenly I didn't know any more if I had really seen or only imagined it, and I wouldn't have been able to find the spot. The next day I walked into a church in Gemona and lit a candle, in case it was a hanged man, after all. For a long time, I was too afraid to set foot in the forest. At some point, a logger al-legedly found a dead man hanging from a tree and the police came; he was past recognition. Some people also described particulars, and there were rumours: who it might have been, where he was and why he did it. Debts, love, sadness – there are enough reasons, if you think about it long enough. Maybe he was a logger; whoever he was, he must have been skilled, to make it up to that branch and then hang himself from it. It was pretty high. It gave me a funny feeling, not being able to talk about it to anyone, to say that I saw him first, since now I couldn't very well tell anyone I'd discovered him and walked away. But my girlfriends wouldn't have been interested any-way; only the men talked about it, as if he had been one of them. For days, conversations revolved around the hanged man, in the bar and sometimes on the bus, as if through talking about it they all wanted to sink their teeth into a piece of this sad story. Maybe it's always like that for men. Lots of talk, little action. I was embarrassed when

153

I found out. I didn't want to hear anything else, and yet here I am talking about it.

GIGI

There were more animals than usual in the village that summer; on some of the alpine pastures the huts and shelters collapsed, making it necessary to return to the valley. All kinds of stories circulated about the dangerous descent – in rain and snow and always with the knowledge that the Earth might begin to quake again. Not all the shepherds are from the valley; some roam the country, hiring themselves out in different regions from one summer to the next. They couldn't stay here, so they went home or searched for work in different regions. That meant I had a little work, and was a shepherd by day. That was fine by me; there would be no wood work for a time, since everyone was busy with the reconstruction. Once in a while the stubborn little German boy followed me; he was good with the animals and he didn't talk too much. But sometimes he would go on, fantasizing about all the things he had in Germany, and his mother. I said nothing, and he would stop talking to himself. Above all, though, he tried to catch vipers. I always worried he would startle an entire nest, but he was skilful and observed everything precisely. When he wanted to get hold of one he moved lightning quick, and let it into the bottle he always had on him. Once he even prevented me from coming into contact with one; he spotted them everywhere, even when they were indistinguishable from the stones they lay on. In the pharmacy they pay you money for them, he said, but I'm not sure he was able to sell them; the pharmacy was in the chief village, where they doubtless had other things to do – the destruction there was great. No hikers or foreigners came around, not even rubberneckers. The rubberneckers were surely making rounds outside, on the main road leading past the entrance to our valley. There was doubtless enough to see there; large towns were said to have been destroyed, with large churches and castles; everything in ruins. Where to go with all the rubble, I sometimes asked myself. Where should it go?

It was a very hot summer, or so it seemed to me; normally I would have been in the forest. I was happy that I could tend to the animals. Herding, milking, being silent or talking to the goats – who never answered, which made it almost like being silent. In the village people argued. Everything was at sixes and sevens. Because ours was the least damaged village in the valley, people complained that we received nothing at all when they brought food, blankets, children's toys, tools, building materials. Everything went to the other villages, people always said. At first everyone helped each other out, but now that they were tired they all saw their own damages. People also stole. And pointed fingers at whoever in the village ended up receiving something after all. And the fear – it didn't go away either. Every roll of thunder brought back the terror. Renovating the houses was slow-going. There was a shortage of everything. Everywhere were heaps of debris. Stones, tiles, roof shingles, splintered beams. The sun shone down, rain fell, grass grew on it, and in the shadows after a couple of months there was already moss. This is how mountains form, I thought. So many broken things lying in heaps, and the weather passes over it, and the debris becomes a small mountain. A landscape, of sorts.

We were lucky; others, less so. And it wasn't only the people. The chickens and pigs needed to eat, too. Who would mow for the people busy repairing their houses?

Who would harvest? At least the corn wasn't ready until late summer. But the hay – now that was something to worry about. I did what I could with a few boys from the village who were already grown and could swing a scythe. Into the panniers, and down to the valley. That was hard work. Sometimes I became dizzy from all the peening and whetting; my head began to drone. But when the sweet grass fell, this whooshing and rustling – that did me good.

FORMATION OF THE MOUNTAINS: SECOND BELIEF

Mountains are the result of tremendous collapses in the Earth's crust, which, in the aftermath of deep tremors, yield to the magnetic pull of Earth's interior. As they collapse, immense masses of material collide; pieces of crust protrude upward every which way, and what is undermost turns uppermost. Ripped out of their moorings in the tumultuous ocean, the land masses collide into one another, the force of the collisions cause startled tectonic plates to fold; depressions and abysms, overthrusts of land plates and strata form. Displacements of oceans and continents loom, humankind helplessly calls out imaginary names into the void. Creative nature's powerful hand thus piles up a range of rocks, and humankind is simply a delicate witness to the forms that arose from tremendous acts. But humans are also talented at speculation, themselves able to assign a story even to the most violent events that took place in their absence.

SILVIA

My mother returned with the soldiers. Everyone watched as she came, it was as if she were from another world, with her elegant shoes and that thin dress and small suitcase. I thought she had returned for good. She had brought us all gifts, even a blouse for my grandmother, although the two of them couldn't stand each other. My grandmother couldn't wear the blouse right away, everything was dirty and full of dust and in shambles, but she hung it in the wardrobe that was already clean and I think she was pleased. It was nice for a few days. My mother helped out a lot, putting things in order and cleaning, and sometimes she sang as she did and was very cheerful. There was a school tent where I went every day, but we didn't have any proper lessons. The soldiers and civil defence officers had brought us all kinds of things for writing and drawing, and in my memory we mostly sang and painted. There was also a small library in the school tent. I have always liked to read. I can remember one book that I read there, about girls on a pony farm in winter. It was about ponies and riding and I don't know what else, only that I really enjoyed the book, but felt cold from all the snow in the story. In the period directly after the earthquake it was very cold here, too. Maybe it's better, then, to read books set in hot climates. I think my mother was also freezing. She always wore such thin dresses, and we couldn't heat the house yet. But she also worked a lot. We went to eat in the large tents, our chimney had collapsed and we still couldn't light a fire for the stove, my father was repairing it but it took time. After all he wasn't a bricklayer. Sometimes they bickered at dinner, or afterwards, if someone made eyes at my mother, then my father became angry. But it always passed, and my father and mother even held hands. The women took turns cleaning up, it was always a group of women and everyone wanted to be with my mother, to hear what she had to say about her work at the seaside. Everyone enjoyed that. They laughed and smoked and hung onto my mother's every word. Why don't you come with me, then, the next time I go? my mother said to one of the women, who in turn became very silent and blushed. A few days later at home she said she had to leave soon, it was only because of the earthquake that she had been able to take vacation time at all. The season was just beginning down there and she would be needed. She wanted to take me with her. My father grew very pale. They argued, but at least they didn't scream, and there weren't any blows either, and I tried not to listen.

The next day her suitcase was packed. During summer vacation you'll come stay with me, she said. At the seaside. I can't remember if I was excited. Summer vacation was almost there. A truck driver took her along down out of the valley, and she waved out the window. The bus wasn't in service yet.

That evening a neighbour came by, my father was outside, every evening he tinkered with his moped in order to get it up and running again, that was the most important thing. The neighbour often teased him about the effort he made with his moped. He always just stood there, hands in his pockets, and watched. Did your firefly leave again? he asked and laughed – I heard it myself. Then there was a muffled bang, as if something heavy had fallen down, and my grandmother bolted out and screamed, Water, she yelled, Water. The neighbour lay on the ground, his face covered in blood. I saw my grandmother cuff my father's ear. He said nothing, just came into the kitchen and got a bowl, and then pumped water in the yard. I didn't want to look out, but I did anyway, I couldn't see much. Only the feet of our neighbour. My father came in, pushing me back into the room. You stay inside, he commanded. I went to bed, and I was so cold, I was afraid that the neighbour was dead. But the next day everything was fine. I saw the neighbour walking in the street below, and my father was very calm.

At the end of the school year, in class we talked about what we wanted to become. Most girls wanted to be saleswomen or hairdressers. I can't remember what the boys wanted to be, but a lot of children also said they wanted to go to Germany or Switzerland. I said I wanted to go to a pony farm. The other children laughed at me and asked if I wanted to become a pony, but I didn't care. I had no clue what I wanted to be; I couldn't imagine an occupation for myself at all.

On the first days of summer vacation I was still at home. I asked: When will I go to the seaside, but my father just said: Soon, and nothing else. I was very excited. Occasionally I played with the other children, either ball or hide-and-seek, and we were allowed to go all the way down to the river to play. At the spot where we went into the water, there was a summer colony with sheds for the livestock, and almost all the cottages had collapsed during the earthquake. But directly by the river you didn't see any of that, you couldn't see our village either, and the view of the mountains was entirely different there than it was around us, sometimes I felt very far from home. You couldn't swim there, there were too many stones in the water.

CARNIVAL

Carnival is the largest celebration in the valley. Day and night, the music plays, and people dance: white masks and dark masks, the tired and the alert, those who stayed and those who went, wordless and without touching, simply part of the music, with its small shifts, changes, dislocations, forever in sight of the partner's mask. The masks must not fall, and the dancing and the music mustn't stop, until the celebration is over – a yearning spinning around itself: for the forgotten, for the ability to forget, until the winter dolls are burnt and – the music playing on, playing faster – the carnival of costumed people in white overgarments with eyeholes and heretic hats is carried in a coffin to the grave.

TONI

Comical things also happened that you could laugh about afterwards. Someone on our road took a cow into their charge, from a neighbour further below in the village, whose shed had collapsed. He put it with his goats; it was tight, but better than nothing, he said. The cow lowed and lowed – perhaps it missed its home. The owner would come every day for milking, and then there was a bit of peace. And she also brought hay. The cow stood close to the door, and one night it nibbled at the light switch. Maybe it also broke loose; I can't remember. It must have been extraordinarily hungry, and the hay wasn't enough. It completely ripped out the switch, all the wires included; the electricity had been back on in the village only for a few days. It received an electrical shock and was half-paralyzed or burnt. That morning the door wouldn't open, because the cow lay in front of it, and the goats were bleating as if everything were in flames. The cow was still alive, but it had to be put down. Fortunately the goats didn't chew on the switch – then the misfortune would have been even greater. Goats are actually much more curious than cows, so that was a miracle, but goats are also clever – cleverer than cows. Maybe they had already learned their lesson from the cow that fell over. Of course

a big fight broke out between the owner and the neighbour. What was to be done? It wasn't anyone's fault, just
another case of bad luck. That's how it was for months.
Afterwards we laughed over the story of the cow that
electrocuted itself, but that was later. Of course I felt bad
for the cow, and the owner. And then no one knew what
to do with the dead animal. Maybe they divided it up and
ate it. At all events, I didn't see anyone come to pick up
the cow. The renderer had to come for dead animals, but
sometimes they were buried and heaped with limestone
on a certain meadow, before the village.

FORMATION OF THE MOUNTAINS:
THIRD BELIEF

Falling comets were ignited by the sun's fire and transformed – melting and solidifying into mountains on
Earth, which consist primarily of granite: a stone that
appears ossified like glass and contains no trace of a
prehistoric creature or organism. All the other elevated
structures of sandstone, slate, limestone and the like are
incidental, occasional formations caused by tremors, surrounding the comet mountains.

ANSELMO

That summer my grandmother's confusion began. Maybe
it came from the earthquake. Every day she went from the
tent up to the house and worked. She was also the first to
return to the house to sleep. She claimed she was being
robbed in the tent. Then she forgot small things. Where
was the jar of coins, where was the twine, or the weed
hoe. And it was always my sister's fault. Then she began
calling us by different names. You *Ansalber*, you, she said

161

to me – and by that she meant something like, *you dickens.* Clear off, you *Ansalber.* My sister was the wimp. But if we ever hurt ourselves, when my sister was sick with a fever and had an upset stomach, our grandmother was right there with her herbs, plantain weed or yarrow and stinging nettle, all kinds. Once my sister had a swelling on her leg: my grandmother put a piece of chewed garlic on it, with her own spit, it was a mush, totally disgusting, but by the next day it was all healed. My father pretended he didn't notice her confusion. After all, she kept working, in the house and in the yard, and she stacked wood as always, not a single hack went amiss. She also butchered as before, we kept a few rabbits and chickens. It wasn't all the time, only on occasion she had days when she looked like a devil.

Once we had moved back into the house, in the evenings, when everything was clean and in order, she set my grandfather a place at the table, as on All Saints' Day. Drink, food. Wine in the glass, bread. The bread always disappeared. The wine remained. I think my sister took the bread – once I heard her get up in the middle of the night. Besides, I saw crumbs in her bed. I didn't say a thing, we just laughed together when our grandmother started up again, setting a place for the dead.

V

'Common limestone. So far, this categorization can
be applied far and wide to most varieties of limestone,
which partly form... large strips of land and entire mountain chains.... Their colours are extraordinarily varied;
every nuance of white, grey, yellow, red, and even black,
in various mixtures and gradations.... The dark grey and
black colours in common limestone are attributable to
coal and bitumen, the latter of which is also recognizable
by the odour emitted by the stone when broken into,
sometimes even by exudations of bitumen or petrole-
um. That explains why such limestones fire white and
gradually fade on the surface, which often appears white
or light grey, while the fresh breakage is black.'
— Carl Friedrich Naumann, *Essentials of Geology* (1850)

MINIERA

Directly at the entrance to the valley a turnoff leads over a bridge and into the rugged mountains, headed for the northside of Monte Plauris. A narrow, cracked road shot through with potholes follows the course of an icy green brook that joins the river shortly before the valley's exit. On the westside of this confluence, pressed into the yellowish cliffs, extends a rugged, long building: a brewery that has not been operated for decades, which once profited from the raging and dependable water of the *torrenti* flowing past, the wild fluctuating brooks. At first glance, the building – marred, perhaps, by so many memorial traces of a World War that took place over a hundred years ago – looks like a military complex.

The small road on the eastern side of the brook leads deep into the valley cut into the hills. At the beginning flowers still bloom on the wayside, individual small butterfly bushes that have propagated from the open valley entrance all the way here. It is a cold valley, turned to the north, and the brook takes on an increasingly frosty colour, a wild brook, that noticeably comes from a certain height. The shadows between the steep hillsides are already long, early in the day. Bordered by tall, dark needle forests and the brook, the road becomes bumpier until eventually it is completely unsurfaced, trickling away between the rocks where a footbridge leads over a brook, to a steep path on the other side. It is a rocky country, a mix of white limestone and darker dolomite, but the bright, the whiteish material predominates; plants are sparse, trees scrubby. The path ascends among scree and spurs of rock, up to a bitumen mine long-shuttered, where the view opens up to gorges and the bright scars of fresh rockslides. Audible everywhere: the water. The mine provided work for more than a century, a risky drudgery

166

in the tunnels to the tarry deposits, the black layers of oil shale pressed between layers of dolomitic limestone, from which the viscous mass that carried the promise of progress was milked: bitumen or asphalt. *Pitch* or *slime*, as it is known in the Bible, the stuff to thank for the success of Noah's ark, and the beginnings of the Tower of Babel, whose bricks were attached using asphalt from the Miocene heights around the Euphrates and the Tigris. The mass is black, smells bitter and pungent and is mildly flammable. Inside the tunnels the extracted material was loaded onto small rail carts, then shot out onto a natural plateau. From there it was brought laboriously downhill, until they reached the other side of the brook, where another set of rails began, which took the bitumen down to the processing plant. There, in the town at the valley exit, the extracted mass was distilled, the clear material separated from the impermeable black in a peculiar self-feeding process, fuelled by the gasses it released. The bitumen boils itself. This produced dead oils, used to operate the streetlamps of Udine, for example, an achievement of progress that the miners themselves probably never set eyes on until they left the valley – exhausted, sick and tired – to look for new work. The streetlights continued to burn after the bitumen ran dry, when it became either comparatively too expensive or laborious to mine. And the miners were left empty-handed, the oily black having penetrated so deeply into every furrow of their skin that it could no longer be washed away, the whites of their eyes still red-veined from the harsh vapours, heaving into their worries, how would they earn their bread? Many of them were *bergfertig*, as they said, *mountain spent*, sick from years of working inside the mountain, where one's sense of day and night and light and dark is lost.

FOUND OBJECT

A photograph, black-and-white with a border, shiny, small, rectangular, a portrait. It shows a young girl. The girl is perhaps six years old. She stands outside in a yard or a lane; the shadows of thin twigs depict themselves on the bright ground beside her, in the overexposed left part of the image one can make out two chickens. In the background, blurry, the figure of a woman, cut off above the hips, her skirt and apron knee-length, a hand reaching for the child. The girl wears a polka-dotted summer dress that buttons down the front. A doll hangs from her right hand, she reaches out her left hand, as if to grab something beside the camera. Her dark hair is braided in two plaits.

MARA

It was always a struggle with my brother. He helped out around the house but often left, heading up to the next village, where the damage was much worse. The men whistled at him as he walked past, laughing, said he should help us out here. He's off to go grind the organ again with his nitwit! they called out. I didn't listen. Your brother has a lover up there who's even dumber than your mother! my neighbour said. Just watch out he doesn't move her into your house!

It was a very hot summer. The house was mostly re-paired in a few weeks, but they said we had to install a few measures to protect us in the event of an earthquake. My brother chased them away, this group of engineers and surveyors who went from door to door. What good will it do me now, after the earthquake, he called out. You guys should have come up with that earlier.

In August there were terrible storms. Our country is

damned, the people said. Here only misfortune prospers. The house trembled in the many thunderclaps. Rain fell in sheets. Our small river became a raging current. Water filled people's tents. Further below in the valley there was a landslide; it acted as a dam, letting rainwater flood the meadows and fields. Corn rotted and beans and potatoes did, too, but luckily we were spared that. After our days in the tent my mother was so calm that I no longer locked her door, but one night she went out in the storm. The next morning I found her on the bench in front of our house. Her wet shirt stuck to her body and her feet were so dirty it looked as if she were wearing shoes. I was so angry I could have slapped her, but I didn't. I cleaned her up and dressed her in a dry shirt. But she was already suffering from hypothermia. It happens quickly to old people. She coughed and developed a fever, and soon it turned into pneumonia, and then she died. In death she was small as a child. The bells rang for her so sweetly, and everyone came to sit vigil by the body. They all barged in to give condolences, because there was food. I stood at the stove the whole time. It was so hot and we were still making do with everything. A candle fell down beside the body, and the women sitting by shrieked: She's alive, she's alive! But that wasn't true. Immediately they said it would bring misfortune. Here anything that's not part of the big plan brings misfortune. But who really knows the big plan ahead of time? Maybe they're just looking for a way to explain all our misfortune.

TONI

In early summer we occasionally went to the river; there were too many of us. The girls stayed on our side, splashing around and giggling, while we boys waded over to the other side, where the bank was steep, a real bluff with a spot you could jump from. It was dangerous, but no one wanted to admit they were afraid. Only one person could jump at a time, because you had to aim precisely for the deepest spot, where there was only space enough for one. Thankfully there was a lot of water that year. We also wanted to show off for the girls. They acted as if they paid us no attention. But if one of us was uneasy and didn't want to jump right away they would laugh and call out: Coward! Coward! Even though they never swam themselves. The water was very cold, I'm sure it was still snow melt from the peaks above. From the water one could see that the cliff had stripes. Nearly black and nearly white, like layers running in wavy lines that looked pasted together. In the cracks small flowers and grasses grew. That's something I never forgot; I still go there sometimes today, nothing about the cliff has changed. It's still striped, whitish and black, but now there are small spruces growing up on the ledge. Less water travels in the river through the valley, it seems; the children no longer jump from up there. I myself wouldn't dare to now.

As time passed some of the other children went to relatives, and my cousin, the German one, was always talking about how his mother would come and take him and his sister to Germany or to the seaside. But she never came. After that he often went off with Goat Gigi, up to the alpine pasture, so no one could ask him when his mother would arrive.

Once I took my camera down to the river, the one my father had given me. It was a Russian device he had bought from a colleague. The device had a name, I can't remember what, but my father pronounced it very proudly when he brought it home. He spelled out the name for me, printed above the lens; he always liked to demonstrate that he could read Russian. My father wanted to teach me how to take photographs, but then the earthquake hit. Luckily nothing happened to the camera. Down by the river I pretended to take pictures, especially of the girls, who shrieked and splashed water on me. One tried to rip the device out of my hand, causing it to fall into the water, at the edge, onto the pebbles. Nothing broke, and I dried it very carefully, and later even took it along to Moscow, and photographed with it there. I have photos aplenty from Moscow.

NATURE

The first photograph from nature was made 150 years before the earthquake. The French chemist Niépce coated a tin plate in asphalt and exposed it to light inside a camera. The exposure lasted hours. Where beams of light met the bitumen, it became hard and insoluble. Once the exposure was complete the plate was rinsed in a solvent that removed everything but the areas touched by light. After the treatment with lavender oil, the photographed outlines and forms, bright and dark, all became manifest. The first photograph from nature made using this method shows the view from Niépce's window onto buildings, crudely granular like a pointillist painting. Niépce named this process heliography.

SILVIA

I had never been on vacation, not even with my parents. I'd been to Gemona, to Udine, but nowhere else. From the seaside town my mother sent me two or three postcards, which I hung over my bed. The sea, the beach, the large hotels – I couldn't picture any of it at all. We didn't have a suitcase for me. My father borrowed one from God knows who, but it was too big, and smelled of mould. My grandmother packed my suitcase, to which I added my card game and my doll, although I hadn't played with it for a long time. The suitcase stood out front below the awning, certainly for two or three days, and every time I walked past it I smelled the mould.

On the day of my departure my father brought me to our neighbour, he had a car and was supposed to take me to Udine, where I would get the bus. It was the car I had slept in after the earthquake, I believe it was red. The entire family rode along, even the boy who had kneed me in the back on the night of the earthquake. I hadn't forgotten that, I couldn't stand him. The mother kept turning around to face me and said: You must be looking forward to the sea? And: That's going to be so nice – at the seaside with mum! She asked me if I also had a bikini and wanted to know what colour it was, and I said: Blue with white polka dots, although I didn't have a bikini at all.

The trip seemed so long, I was so excited. In Udine we got lost and I missed the bus. My mother had come from her seaside town to meet me and was waiting for us, she had taken the day off. She was pretty nervous when we finally arrived, she was afraid something had happened to us. We had to wait quite a while for the next bus. This suitcase is an embarrassment, she said. A whale of a thing, and it stinks. Did you bring along some rubble from up there? I wasn't sure if it was supposed to be a joke or if she was mad, but then my mother laughed, and so did I. It was very hot. We ate an ice cream near the bus station, and afterwards I felt nauseous. On the bus I looked out the window and waited for the sea. The sky was grey, altogether everything was grey, that's how I remember it, the flatland, the large fields. Factories. You saw nothing of the

172

earthquake. On the way my mother pointed into the distance out the windshield, you could already see the town, the hotels that sprung up like towers. I couldn't make out the sea yet.

When we arrived there was a thunderstorm. The wind swept dust through the streets and the trees leaned, there was thunder. People held tight to their sunhats and ran to the hotels. We had just made it under the roof when it began to rain.

The hotel where my mother worked was not one of the tall ones, but had only four or five floors. She shared a room with a colleague and was allowed to put an extra bed in the room for me. We didn't have much space. The floor was cool and smooth, of a black-and-white dappled stone. It was cold on my feet. You'll get used to it, my mother said. People live differently here than in the mountains. Here there is the sea, and summer is hot.

Our window faced the courtyard, and at the very bottom was the kitchen exit, where all the trashcans were. My mother cursed the stinking suitcase, she immediately washed all my things in the sink and took the suitcase away. I wore one of her nightgowns to bed. Her colleague's name was Luigia, she was very funny, I haven't forgotten her. The rain never stopped, but we went to the sea anyway, with Luigia, walking very close to the houses until we reached a spot where one could slip between the fence and the gazebos down to the beach. The sea was full of white caps and waves, at first it made me nervous. Now I'm at the sea, I thought, I can still remember the feeling today. Everything in that town by the sea was new to me, the colourful lights decorating the restaurants, music everywhere. We ate pizza, and then I had to go to bed. Luigia gave me the rest of her pink nail polish, she had bought a new bottle. As I lay in bed Luigia and my mother painted their nails and talked quietly. But I still couldn't sleep, even after the light was turned off. The cook and the kitchen help stood in the small courtyard, smoking and talking, and I heard the lid of the trash can clatter, and a flickering light travelled from the other side of the courtyard all the way into our room. In this light the small black dapples on the floor appeared to dance. Music came from somewhere. I had never slept in the midst of such noise. Sounds came from all sides, from below and above, through the stone floor. Everything was different. But I wasn't homesick.

FOUND OBJECT

A photograph, colour, glossy, rectangular, medium scale, landscape format. Two children, eight, nine, ten years old, standing on the bank of a river. One can see a row of poplars in the background, on the other bank flatland, a smokestack. The sky is pale. The light bright and without shadow. They're both wearing shorts and sleeveless striped gym shirts. One blue, the other red. Dark hair clipped short, both of them. At the edge of the image, the corner of a blanket in the grass. Behind it a path, a blue car. Both children are holding sticks, pointing them at the camera. One can make out a snake at the end of one stick, the other is bare. The smaller child with the bare stick looks to the side, the other child looks into the camera and laughs. The colours are tinged red.

GIGI

When I think back on it today, it seems to me that that summer was very hot. The heat often stood in the valley; nothing moved, the animals were stubborn, and at times the birds screamed so shrilly, up high in the sky. That summer many people went crazy I think – they simply lost their minds – and I'm not sure if it was because of the earthquake or the strange weather, or whether this disquiet pervaded the world of the valley. There was a lot of arguing in the heat, and heartache. And in the middle of all this disquiet, people came from below, from outside – even politicians – and gave talks and praised us here in the valley, because we were so hardworking and brave. They had assistants who walked ahead of them, clearing out of the way whatever lay around – wooden boards and stones – and calling over anyone they thought would cut a good figure in a picture with the politicians. Whenever the politicians came, several photographers were in tow, along with reporters, and to take a picture with the people who were actually from here, the earthquake victims – that was a must, although here things weren't even that bad. They wanted me to be in a picture too, with my goats – I should be on one side of the politician, with my goats, and a bricklayer on the other side – but I said no, and they found someone else. Later someone from the village came to show me the picture from the newspaper, there's a goat's rump in it – we had a laugh. We were actually making good progress, but the mood was so bitter, the tension so thick, as the saying goes, you could cut it with a knife. Two cows died that summer, that had never happened before. Usually people tended to their cattle better than to their children, they always said, because the cattle sustained them. And the children needed sustaining, you could say. Sometimes it was as if different plants grew that summer, different herbs, and that's how they poisoned themselves, the animals.

Later that summer the mad woman died – the one who could spoil my milk and cheese just by laughing, at least sometimes. It was terrible: she lost her way and they found her, already half-rotten in a gorge; it was the vultures that gave her away, someone said, because back then we still had vultures.

FOUND OBJECT
A photograph, colour, no border, glossy, medium scale, rectangular, landscape format. A young woman sits on a light blue Vespa and smiles at the camera. The Vespa stands in a row of scooters, all the same kind – red, silver, white – on display for sale. The young woman wears a pale yellow summer mini-dress, sleeveless, and sunglasses. Her hair is auburn, curly, short. The Vespa and the young woman cast a shadow on the asphalt. At the shop door stands a man with a handlebar moustache. The large display window reflects the traffic and also a man, who stands on the forecourt of the shop and takes the photograph.

LINA
For a few years now I've been selling things from my garden, garlic and radishes and herbs. And slippers that I make in winter. Everything has a use. When I have enough things together I sell them on the side of the road, near Venzone. My youngest sister drives me there, I never learned to drive. She has a car, she works further away. In a factory that produces cardboard boxes. Her hands are always chafed. On Saturdays she smears her hands in honey and pulls on an old pair of gloves, she sits like this on the sofa and does nothing until the afternoon. Then she fixes herself up, and her boyfriend comes to take her out on his motorcycle. He is Yugoslavian, from Croatia,

176

he says, and he has a red rose tattooed on his arm. My sister's name is Maria-Rosa, and he claims he got the tattoo for her, but he must have already had it when they met, they haven't known each other that long. He told someone else in the village that he's a gardener who specializes in roses. He's from the seaside and says he wants to take Maria-Rosa away to the seaside. He already built the house. He shouldn't do it unless he's good to her and can put food on the table. He showed me pictures of his home, they made a good impression. Except that the houses are shabby, like the ones they built here after the earthquake. They all learned that in Germany, my husband said to me once, when he saw a picture. He must know.

My sister lets me out on the main road before Venzone, and I carry my things in a pannier to the place where I set up my little stand. The stand is only a few wooden crates, which I hide again in the afternoon, in the bush beside the road. Some days there is a lot of traffic, especially in summer when vacationers also drive past. I stand on the side where they head home, it's practical. Sometimes truck drivers also stop and act like they want to buy something. A few of them are also nice, one gave me a small bottle of perfume once. Just because. The perfume stank, You smell like a brothel, my brother said. I dumped the perfume, the little bottle I still have. People like the pannier, they think it's so old-fashioned. As if everything here were as it was a hundred, two hundred years ago. Even if they look down on us otherwise. Once I was in town, talking to a woman from the village, and a woman walking past said: Why do you talk so ugly? People name things in various ways, and in doing so everyone has their own feelings.

Occasionally tourists get out to take a picture of me. Some ask first, others don't. If they ask, I make a friendly face, otherwise I don't. What will become of me in these pictures, I wonder. Where do I lie around, with my pannier, abroad in the houses of stranger? I never went abroad; my husband always asked if I wanted to come along, he could get me a job, but I never wanted to. Maybe I'll regret that one day, I don't know. Someone told me that it was so beautiful, my stand with the cathedral and the mountains in the background. I told my sister and she laughed. Don't make anything of it, she said, for them you're just like a stone. I have kept only a single photograph of myself, from my wedding. Back then someone from the newspaper came and photographed us. I still like the picture, the guy came all the way back to bring us a copy, and not just the newspaper. Now I'm twice as old, it occurs to me today, twice as old, but in my memory the first half of my life is much longer than the second. As if the Earth spun faster after the earthquake. I also made it into other photographs, at village parties and family celebrations, where people are always quick to snap shots, but I never liked these pictures of me, I threw them away whenever someone brought me one, I didn't even want to keep them in a drawer.

On the other side of the river, towering directly across from my stand is the mountain under which the first earthquake lay, supposedly directly below it, or even inside of it. Here everything was completely destroyed. Many things were rebuilt, but the landscape doesn't forget what happens to it, there are ruins and the rubble of houses everywhere, from some of which trees and bushes are already growing, ivy creeping over it. Sometimes I wish I could say something to the mountain, when I stand there all alone and no one is listening. For example: You just keep quiet, nothing like that ever again. But it's too late. The world all around has changed.

RETINA

Years before his successful experiment of exposing an asphalt-coated tin plate, Niépce attempted to expose paper coated with silver salts. When exposed to the sun, silver salts turn black. The coated papers were laid in a camera obscura and exposed to the incidence of light. The first depiction by light exposure was thus made long before the invention of heliography. It was the invert image of a view from the window, but the picture disappeared as soon as the sheet was exposed to sunlight, since the coated paper turned completely black. Niépce called these fleeting negatives *retinas*.

SILVIA

While my mother worked I stayed in the hotel or nearby, until she was finished. At first it was odd, all the strangers and just that small room of ours. All the cars and mopeds outside, the noise. But I grew to like it. I ate breakfast all by myself at a table for the attendants. It stood halfway behind a dividing wall, beside the entrance to the kitchen. I could watch the guests eat breakfast, families and elderly people. Most of them were foreigners. One married couple had a small dog that sat below the table. Like a bewitched human child, that's how they treated it. The waiters were all nice to me, and so was the man at the reception desk. Everyone always wanted to hear about the earthquake. Whether my house had been completely destroyed, whether I'd been buried beneath rubble, whether people around us had died. What we were going to do now, whether everything would be rebuilt. What should I have said? If I could answer the question I told the truth, if not sometimes I fibbed or made something up, or said: Don't know. The man at the reception desk was named

Giovanni but called himself Johnny, so the foreigners would have an easier time pronouncing his name. I always called him Johnny. He had a small television set in his office behind the reception desk, where I was allowed to watch whatever I wanted. At home usually only a single channel worked, there was too much interference for the others. I watched all kinds of things on television there, fashion shows and romance movies, and cartoons. Giovanni watched with me occasionally, when work was quiet, he always wanted to watch sports, and from time to time he would start on the earthquake. But I was happy to tell him about it, although I occasionally fibbed to him, too.

My mother was a chambermaid in the hotel. She had to tidy rooms, clean bathrooms, make beds and change sheets when people left. The first few days I wanted to help her, but that just made her nervous. Every room had a sink, and some also had bathrooms. On the sink she placed a fresh soap, small soaps formed like shells, in light yellow and blue, and pink. Sometimes I stole them, when I saw the wagon with towels and sheets in the hall. The dishes with soap were there too. I hid them in one of my socks, but at some point my secret came out, and my mum tried to be stern with me. Luigia just laughed. Don't get caught, my mother said, and began to laugh herself.

In the afternoon I would sit with the chambermaids and waiters at the table behind the dividing wall, after all the guests had been served. That was always fun, they laughed a lot and joked about the guests. And about Johnny. I felt bad for him: I like him a lot, I said. Oh my, one of the women said, you like Johnny a lot? Don't get your hopes up, he swings the other way. And then they all broke into laughter again, and I was embarrassed.

I was allowed to play outside, too, in the street near

the hotel. I had brought along my jump rope. Most of the time I just looked around. There was always a lot going on. Once there was an accident, two cars crashed into each other, it made a loud bang. The traffic police arrived immediately and stood around everywhere. The drivers screamed at each other, the police surveyed the damage. The cars were damaged, but they still ran. And then there was a big commotion when the television reporters arrived. Everyone crowded around for a look. We had to stand outside before the caution tape, only a few men were allowed to remain sitting in the bar. Someone was allowed to decide exactly who could stay seated and who had to leave. Someone made an announcement with a megaphone, asking if someone could move their small three-wheeled Piaggio Ape, it was in the way. But no one came. Then a woman got out of a car and everyone whistled and called out, Mia! Mia! and clapped. She was a famous pop singer, I also knew her, from television. She wore a long dress and sauntered about, pretending to sing. Maybe she really was singing, I couldn't hear. She was led around here and there, into the bar, onto a side street, the cameramen always in tow. The traffic police all came over and watched, too. Of course they were able to cut in. It was actually boring. I went back to the hotel and told Giovanni about it; he was very interested. He even ran outside for a moment to catch sight of it and get her autograph. In the meantime I had to stand at the reception desk and if someone came, politely say: Signor Johnny is tied up at the moment, he'll be with you shortly. I was so nervous someone would come, to this day I remember the sentence.

In the evening we went to the beach. But not to the expensive beach with reclining armchairs and umbrellas. We went to a wild beach, where you didn't have to pay a thing. It was pretty far away, through a pine forest. Later my mother borrowed a Vespa from someone in order to take me to the beach. The drive was actually the nicest part, as I sat on the back of the Vespa and held onto her tight. Nicer than the beach itself. There were always so many dogs walking around there and I once stepped on a piece of glass; we even had to go to the first-aid station the next day, and they bandaged my foot, because it had become infected. My mother liked to be at the beach. She liked to lay in the sand, and she liked to look at the sea and would turn her small transistor radio on and listen to pop music. She could go on and on with Luigia about pop singers, but she had done that at home, too.

Once she showed me the mountains, you could see them from a spot on the beach, behind the pine forest. That was strange. At first I didn't believe her. I felt so far away from home. Where is our valley? I asked her. You can't see it from here, she said, after all, there are mountains in front of it.

FOUND OBJECT

A photograph, black-and-white, a white border with rough edges, matte. Square, small scale. A young man in a dark turtleneck and wide dark trousers stands in front of a building. Behind him are two high, bright pillars supporting a large balcony, on the right side a building addition. Art nouveau. On the gable above the balcony are the letters – difficult to make out – OVINCIALE. It is a bright day. The man casts a shadow on the ground in front of the pillared entrance. Behind the bright pillars it is dark. Thrown over the man's shoulder is a white bundle that can be taken for a jacket at first glance. A casual summer blazer. He looks calmly at the camera, somewhat

182

rigid, his posture stiff as well. His face round. His body looks skinny. His hair dark, his hairline far receded, his forehead large and white.

LINA

One day crazy Milena was gone. It was afternoon when her husband came to me, a mess. This morning everything was still fine, he said. She had taken the pannier out of the shed and said: I'm going up to the mountain pasture. He just laughed and took it for a joke – maybe she made jokes like that sometimes, I don't know. At any rate, she was gone. A few people even saw her, crossing the river with the pannier on her hunch. All afternoon they searched for her, until it was dark. The next day someone went down out of the valley and sent a telegram to her sons. Both of them abroad. The police came, a few Alpini searched alongside them, then her sons arrived too. Which pasture? the police officers asked, and her husband said: I don't know, I'm not from here.

It was very hot. And this disappearance, it lay like a dark cloud over everything, even over the people still living in tents. Everyone thought: In this heat, how will anyone find her? Crazy Milena. In what condition?

Her husband was so distraught he lost his mind. No one could calm him. When his sons set out on their search, he walked with them to the rock of the dead, and there he remained, standing in the road, holding in his hands before his stomach the framed wedding photograph of Milena and him, like the key to a hidden object puzzle, so everyone could see it, and yet no one passed by – at most some truckers, a few cars. And no one would have been able to recognize her from the photo, anyway: she was a young woman in a wedding dress, wearing a veil, it was before the war. Someone from the neighbourhood came by and took pity on him, persuaded him to get into his car and took him home. Then he sat there on the bench, holding the picture on his lap. I brought him something to eat and drink, and with time he improved, he understood she must be dead.

On the fourth or fifth day they found the pannier, set down neatly beside the trail. Far away from here, across the valley. Quite far up, hours away. And on the other side of the path, across from where her pannier stood, the land dropped deeply into a gorge, where she lay.

Her sons lifted her out, but it would not have been possible without the Alpini. With ropes and hooks they tried until it worked. She was grossly injured. And dead for days. What should they have done? They put her in the pannier and carried her down like that, back to the village. You could see them coming from far away, the one son carrying the pannier on his back. Her husband must have sensed it, even if he couldn't see it, he ran off and then tripped over a board that lay in the way; someone helped him up and took him into the house where they treated the wound. Of course they didn't want him to see his wife, but it took a long time: a doctor had to come, and the police, and then a hearse. In a sheet metal coffin, someone explained: that is how they transport a corpse that is already decomposing. God only knows where he got that from, but maybe it was true.

It was a large funeral, despite the heat and all this misery. The sons carried the coffin, but a real coffin, of wood, and it was a beautiful funeral despite everything, even a small chorus sang, and it was solemn.

CORROSION

Niépce sought a process for etching an image onto a plate by means of the sun. He investigated the effect of light on various acids with the hope of finding one that would corrode when exposed to light. He had in mind a principle of coating limestone with acids whose effect depended on the intensity of the incidence of light and which as a result would etch the likeness into the stone according to the various translucencies on the surface of the projected image. But light does cause acids to corrode, and his plan could not be realized. From this process, however, he learned that under the influence of light even an invisible process can cause an image to emerge in a chemical reaction.

OLGA

In June my cousins came. Back then they worked in Austria, I think. Anyway, they were abroad. They arrived and were immediately angry, because everything was still in such a state of chaos. They collected millions for you out there, and yet here you wouldn't even know it! That was the first thing they said. But then they got to work, and soon we could move back into the house. I cleaned and washed and tidied up everything, since I didn't have to work. The little cat that I'd found during the earthquake came around every evening, or at least I thought it was the same one. I fed it when no one was looking; I wanted it to stay. I also thought its arrival was a good omen. It must have sensed that our house stood secure. In the evening I was afraid to lie down in bed, but it got better with time. Everyone was afraid. At first some people slept in their yards, then they carried their mattresses into their hallways, then further into the house. As if slowly drawing nearer to a dangerous animal. But what was the animal in this equation? The poor houses couldn't do anything about it.

One evening I heard my aunt in the kitchen, saying to her sons: Take Olga with you, when you go back. Here there's nothing left for her.

At first it hit me like lightning – she didn't know I was listening. But then I became very excited. I would have gladly left. I waited for them to say something, but didn't bring it up myself. In the evenings I would prick my ears towards the kitchen, but they never discussed it again. I thought about it: What do I want to take with me? What will I wear? And where was my suitcase? Since we had arrived from Venezuela I hadn't used it. I didn't want to ask anyone, and searched for it myself. A state of chaos still reigned. In the end I found it – absolutely filthy – outside in the shed, where my cousins had brought everything from the attic. It was a small brown suitcase with a checked lining and two straps that buckled shut. I cleaned it up and as I did, one of my cousins saw me, and laughed. At dinner he said: I think Olga wants to get out of town, and everyone poked fun at me. Maybe she's in love with a soldier, my other cousin said right away, and my father turned bright red, angered by their dumb jokes. Tucked into one of the interior pockets was an old newspaper clipping. In Venezuela there was an Italian newspaper, and they wrote about the shoe factory. In the centre of the article was a photograph of a group of workers, my parents among them, my sweet mother and my father, and they smiled, cheerful as children in the picture. Someone had circled their heads for me with a pen, that's why I found them right away. They didn't know what life had in store for them. Once the clean suitcase stood in my room, I wanted to get away even more – it

186

didn't matter where to, I just wanted to see something, to get out there.

But the subject of them taking me along was never raised again, no matter how hard I pricked my ears to listen in on their evening talks. Once their vacation was over, my cousins disappeared, without a word of goodbye. Nice vacation, they said, every bone in our bodies hurts – but they didn't mention that it was their last evening, and they must have left very early the next morning.

The little cat gave me joy; I would have been sad to leave her. She caught everything that moved. She was a savage. One day she brought a snake into the yard. A young *carbon*. She held it between her teeth, the snake all the while beating its tail as if it were a whip, it looked scary. The cat conducted herself very smartly, evading the snake until the snake at last managed to strike her after all, and the cat let it fall, and the snake darted away like a bolt of lightning, beneath the rubble pile lying near the gate. Everything that had accumulated as we straightened up and renovated. Parts of the old balcony were there, and chunks of wall. On the stone in the yard the snake had left behind a trail of blood, a zigzag. For hours, the cat sat in front of the rubble pile, waiting for the snake to emerge – but surely it had found another way out and was already back home, somewhere cool, in the shadows, in the dampness, that's where they like to live, the black *carbons*.

In August there was a funeral. Two, actually. Both for old women no longer right in the head. So good for her daughter, everyone said about the one woman, and I don't think anyone mourned her. The other woman lost her way in the forest and plummeted. That was sad. Her husband cried, as did her sons; the way they carried her coffin to the grave was very moving. Two girls from the choir asked me to sing with them at the cemetery. It had been so long since I'd last sung, but no one else wanted to do it. What should we sing? we asked the dead woman's daughter. She requested Riba Faronika. But we talked her out of it. Your mother was old, we said, and you aren't a young mother, there are no children to speak of. She agreed, and we chose a Song of Canin, that always works. The mountain is always there. We practised a few times, just the three of us. It was very beautiful at the cemetery. The coffin was small, small enough for a child, a sad sight. They said she gave birth to so many children, and then in death she herself was once again a child. At the other funeral we also sang the Song of Canin.

FOUND OBJECT

A photograph, black-and-white, matte with a border, medium scale, rectangular, portrait format. Three women and a man working in a field. The women are wearing dark stockings and bandanas, skirts, jumpers; the man is wearing an undershirt and wide trousers with suspenders. Two of the women and the man are bent over the field with their hoes. They're working, and the outline of their arms moving the hoes is slightly out of focus. The third woman, nearest the camera, has drawn herself up. In her one hand she holds the shaft of the hoe, in the other, a large white stone, as if she had just harvested it. She's laughing. The sun shines brightly on the field. It is spring, the willowish trees lining the field have a few leaves. Towering in the background is a snow-capped mountain. Two bottles lie in the grass on the edge of the field. Straight furrows run through the field. The soil is riddled with stones. On the hillside above the laughing woman with the stone, projecting into the image is the

188

edge of a house, the corner of a wooden balcony, above it a wooden gable.

ANSELMO

Whenever I went around with Goat Gigi he explained and showed me things that I remember to this day. The names of flowers and which ones the goats must not eat and why. He also knew many birds by name. Once, up on the alpine pasture he suddenly said: Listen to that! He was talking about a quiet rasping noise, *krek krek, krek krek.* It's your bird, he whispered. I never would have thought a bird could sound like that, at first I took it for a joke. But he actually never joked. Sure, he could be strange, and sometimes that was funny, but jokes – they weren't for him. Corncrake was the bird's name, but as Gigi told me later, in some parts it is called King of the Quail. That was odd, since my last name means quail. I knew about quails, some people kept them in cages, just as we kept rabbits. After that I often listened out for the bird, but heard it only at night, extremely far away, very faint. Once as a joke I said to my sister and grandmother: I don't want to be named Quail any more – call me King of the Quail. My grandmother laughed: a rare occurrence, at least after the earthquake. She told us about how King of the Quail got its name. In truth it is an unremarkable bird, there's nothing kingly about it. Everyone just called it krek-krek, after its call. But one day a farmer caught one that he mistook for a quail. Back at the yard he put it in a cage, together with his other quails. Oh that krek-krek, the quails said, he's just what was missing around here. I'll lead you to freedom! the krek-krek said. But then you'll have to make me king. The quails agreed to it. That evening the farmer stuck his hand in the cage to feel the birds to determine who would

189

fatten up quickest. He was already looking forward to the first roast quail. The krek-krek nipped him hard in the finger, its beak much stronger than a quail's. The farmer screamed and pulled back his hand, then he rumbled into the house to get a knife to slaughter the krek-krek immediately. But he forgot to close the door to the cage, and at once all the birds were outside in the open, and when the farmer returned with his knife, the cage was empty. The quails stuck to their promise and named the krek-krek King of the Quails, and that satisfied him. He didn't need anything else, just a posh name.

I thought it was a nice story, but my sister immediately fired back. Then you have to lead us out of our cage, before you can be King of the Quails, she said, and the high mood was good as gone, and our grandmother was back to her bitter self.

By the end of summer vacation our house was repaired. My father took everything that could be burnt, yet wasn't suitable for the woodstove, out back to the meadow behind our house and wanted to build a fire. He liked building fires, the neighbours would come and grouse whenever the wind blew smoke over to them. Get the hell out, you gypsy! one yelled sometimes, when he was angry, Go back to Germany with your band! But my father didn't care, and by the next day it was completely forgotten, as if the neighbour had never said it at all. Only I held onto it. The fire smelled terrible, God knows what he burned. My sister and I walked around the fire, catching burning tatters of ashes – we used two old dip nets from the shed, it was fun, I still remember it today. My father was also in a good mood. In the end he went into the house and got a box and tossed the contents on the fire, and the flames became very small, but it smouldered and stank so terribly that it burnt my eyes. I caught an ashen tatter and saw that it was a photograph. It was burnt only on one side, my mother was in the photograph, heavily made up with upswept hair; they were incinerated up to their stomachs. Throw it back in the fire! my father scolded, and I threw it back. I think on that evening my father burned everything that he still had from Germany, including photographs of us, and that's why it stank and smouldered as it did. At any rate I never found the photographs again.

FOUND OBJECT

Instant photograph, in colour with a border, glossy, square. Three figures in costume, wearing long white robes and under that lace stockings and buckled shoes. On their heads they wear enormous bonnets, adorned with paper flowers, and around their hips, wide belts. The central figure has hidden her face with colourful ribbons that hang from the bonnet. They stand in the scrawny winter grass behind a fieldstone wall, the stones whitish, yellowish, grey, veined, broken. Between the stones are dark cavities, tiny. A bluish veil spreads across the image, the contours are not quite crisp, the background is streaked, the upper edge exhibits the shading of blemish, due perhaps to an exposure time inappropriate for the light and temperature conditions.

MARA

After the funeral my brother moved in his sweetheart. And he booked the wedding. She wasn't stupid at all, just mute. She couldn't get a word out. But she was so deft with her hands I could hardly believe it, it was like witchcraft. She could sew and darn and kill a chicken like no

191

one else, she was fast as all get-out. The chicken's head lay on the ground before the animal was able to open its beak and screech. It was good to have her around, it made everything easier.

She was always starved for my brother. In the middle of her work she would stare at him, when he fixed something outside, by the window, her lower lip hanging totally askew from hunger, her gaze so vacant, and then they disappeared behind the house, and afterwards everything was good again, and she continued working. Luna, my brother called her. I liked her a lot. We worked together in the yard and out in the field. She was like lightning at sorting beans. By the time I turned around she had practically removed the beans from the pods and divided them into three small piles, according to size. And the foul ones lay in a small pile on the side. Extremely accurate in all she did. How she smiled, whenever she realized she'd done a good job.

We also selected the image for my mother's grave together. There weren't many pictures to choose from. Who would have photographed my mother? We chose one that we had received as a gift. A photographer walked around here one summer, asking if he could photograph people. Striking heads, he said, I would like to photograph the local striking heads. Apparently that was his speciality. He saw my mother sitting on the bench, so he came into the yard. She was already muddled back then, but well-behaved and friendly; maybe it was on one of those days when she spoke to her lost children. He sent me inside; it was better I wasn't there. I watched through the kitchen window, secretly. He set up all his equipment, talking to her all the while, but my mother didn't notice a thing. Then he handed her a small bouquet of flowers that he had quickly picked on the hillside, before the gate. She held the flowers out in front of her and sat very still, as if she knew exactly what it was about. Surely a year passed before he came by again, at which point I had forgotten it entirely. My mother sat on the small bench outside and greeted him as if he were an old acquaintance, and she giggled to herself when he showed her the picture. We didn't have to pay a dime. I found it very austere, the picture, she looks really old in it, but you couldn't tell from looking at her that she was so muddled. Or hardly at all. And the small bouquet of flowers was a nice touch. Yet it was austere. But one could get used to it. And that's what we chose for the gravestone.

VAPOURS

Niépce's method of heliography was held in low esteem. They laughed at how cumbersome it was. A few years later he developed a new process involving polished, bitumen-coated silver plates. He exposed the bitumen to iodine vapours. This method enabled him to produce high-contrast, coarse-grained photographs on metal plates. The exposure time consisted of several days in direct sunlight.

SILVIA

In the evenings we walked around a lot, with Luigia and with my mother's other co-workers. They always did themselves up first. Luigia showed me how to paint my nails. My mother even bought me a dress for our evening strolls. It was a bit too large, but I wore it anyway. It was red. My mother usually wanted to ride bumper cars. I think the man who worked there liked her, the one who sold the tickets, he always tried to put his arm around her.

193

We were allowed to ride for free, but I didn't like it when the cars crashed together and everyone shrieked. More than anything else I enjoyed simply walking around. Every evening was like a holiday, with all the music and the lights, and we ate ice cream and went out on the long pier over the sea, where there was always a lot going on. Occasionally you could see the mountains, still red and orange from the sunset.

For a time I had a friend at the hotel who was also named Silvia. She was from Germany, but spoke a bit of Italian. At first I found the way she spoke strange, but then I got used to it. They just don't want to admit that they're Italians, my mother said. She became angry when I began to speak like the other Silvia. Don't talk like a nitwit, she snarled at me.

A few times the other Silvia and her mother took me along to the beach, when her father didn't want to go. I heard them at the breakfast table, squabbling in Italian, because he never wanted to go to the beach, meaning they had paid for his lounge chair in vain. Then take the earthquake girl with you, he said. They had a place on an expensive beach, the beach chairs and umbrellas stood in a very straight row and there was a small changing booth where I should have put on my bathing suit, but I already had it on under my dress. Good for me, because the booth smelled like pee. They also invited me to eat with them at their table a few times, but they too wanted to hear only about the earthquake. Maybe we can pass by on our drive back, the father said. We could have a look at it, that's not something you see every day. When they wanted to talk alone they sent us away, and we went to Giovanni to watch television. He pretended he didn't believe that we were both named Silvia, and joked about it. But you don't look alike at all! he said at first. Such was the nature of his jokes, and no one laughed as hard as he did.

The other Silvia had an instant camera that her uncle had given her for her birthday, as she mentioned over and over – all the way from America, I think. I had never seen one before. The camera was pretty big and white, with a colourful stripe down the middle. A white camera, I remember that as if it were yesterday! My mother and Luigia didn't believe it until they saw it. Silvia always wore it around her neck when she wasn't on the beach. She wasn't allowed to take the camera there, because of the sand. But when we were allowed to wander through the streets a bit or go out for ice cream, she always brought her camera along. Take a picture already, I said to her, but at first she didn't want to. I have to be very careful about taking pictures, she said. It's so expensive. But then she took one of me, by the fountain where the female pop star had sauntered about. After she snapped it, the photograph shot out the front, all on its own. At first you couldn't see a thing, and then the image gradually appeared. Then we continued to photograph, taking turns – it was a lot of fun – and eventually the film was used up. But the pictures were nice, even if everything did look different than in reality. The other Silvia gave me the first picture she took of me, which came out somewhat crooked. I'm wearing my new dress, the red one for evenings, although it's only afternoon. And I have an ice cream cone in my hand. I'm not sure if I still have the photo somewhere. I don't think so.

FOUND ITEM
A photograph, black-and-white with a border, medium scale, rectangular, landscape format. A group of five

young men in fur-lined leather jackets and fur hats, half-crouching in the snow, their arms around one another's shoulders, grinning broadly, the one in the middle having unbuttoned his fur jacket and his shirt below, so that one can see his sparse chest hair, a cross on a chain resting on it. In front of them a bottle lies in the snow, the man in the middle and the young man beside him have their right leg stretched out as if in a Cossack dance. Behind the group is a construction site in the snow. The sky is overcast. On the reverse, written in pen: *Amici miei*. The writing stands out faintly in relief on the front side.

SILVIA

At the end of summer vacation there was an open-air dance. A dance band was supposed to come and play on a square near the beach. Every evening my mother and Luigia talked about what they would wear. A waitress who lived on our floor had brought a small sewing machine, and all the women wanted to tailor themselves something, or alter or embellish what they already had. Until then I didn't know that my mother could sew. She made herself a very beautiful dress with a wide skirt, in turquoise. Luigia made herself a similar one, in orange. I think there were eight of us in our corridor. Nine including myself. In their new dresses, the women began to practise dances, in their rooms and in the corridor; not just my mother and Luigia, but other women as well. They couldn't find the right music on the radio, so one of them always sang or hummed a melody in the background. A different woman would announce between the songs: Waltz! Polka! Mazurka! And the dance changed. I sat on a chair by the open door of our room and watched. At the end I clapped.

I actually should not have gone: I should have stayed with Giovanni and watched television, before going to bed alone. But Giovanni wanted to go to the dance himself, it was his evening off. That's how it came to be that I went along. The dancefloor was round, and encircled by stone benches where one sat as if on a set of stairs. I had to sit pretty high up and promise my mother I wouldn't leave. Only when Giovanni went back to the hotel was I allowed to go with him. There were other children besides me there, but they were allowed to walk around, that town was their home. Luckily there were no storms that evening, everyone had worried about that. When the orchestra walked on stage everyone clapped and whistled and hooted. A group of only men played instruments, and one woman sang. The men all wore the same white glittering shirts or jackets, and the woman had on a mini dress, in blue glitter. At the start of every song people clapped before they began to dance; many people also sang along. Back home in the valley I had already seen dances – I could even dance already myself – but that was different. The music was so different, as was the way of dancing: in pairs with their arms around each other. I saw my mother dance with the bumper car man, and with other men I didn't know. Luigia mostly danced with the breakfast waiter from our hotel. At the end they sang a song called 'Ciao Ciao Mare'. Everyone knew the song and sang along. The woman sang with one of the musicians, and when they sang *ciao ciao*, all the dancers and everyone in the audience had to wave, and at *mare* move a hand before them, like a snake: this was supposed to represent the waves and the ocean. I joined in, I sang along, too, it was easy.

A few days later summer vacation came to an end. I had to go back home. My mother bought me a new, green suitcase. She packed it beautifully, and folded all of my things, and Luigia gave me the rest of her new nail polish. I nearly forgot my doll. My mother placed a fat white envelope in one of the zippered pockets of my suitcase. Give this to dad, she said. I'll come in the autumn. When everything here is done. We ate pizza and went to the beach and sang *Ciao Ciao Mare*, and the next day my mum brought me to Udine, and from there I rode the bus – the bus that went all the way into the valley – alone. I looked out the window and watched the mountains move ever closer. They looked purple, purple and grey, and so steep and rocky, as if no one would ever be able to climb them.

My father and my grandmother were waiting for me at the square behind the cemetery where the bus stopped. They were happy to have me back home. They said nothing about the suitcase. My legs were very shaky from sitting so long in the bus.

VI

'The cases in which the seismic movement exhausts itself for a long period by one violent shock...are among the rare exceptions. Much more frequent is the occurrence of a whole series of earthquakes, of varying intensity, accompanied or not by subterranean rumbling. Sometimes indeed the maximum intensity moves from place to place along a definite line...'
— Eduard Suess, *The Face of the Earth*, vol. 1 (1892)

FOLIAGE

It is a sunny morning at the entrance to the valley, late September, and already cold. The mountains are veiled in thin clouds, the river is turquoise and cold at the confluence with the wide, white brook that flows out of the bitumen mine-valley. At the foot of the Plauris Massif the waters ripple into one another, swaying westward, bound out of the valley. A cloud casts a thin shadow on the walls of the entrance to the long disused brewery that is squeezed into the cliff. The brewery was once famous for its beer, fermented only here in these rock caves, in the damp shadows of the limestone formations shot through with veins of oil shale – but that was long ago. The ease of the plain won out over the toils of remote cragginess.

The summer birds are long gone. Nightjars, swifts, corncrakes – all gone since August. The snakes lie semi-rigid, sheltering from the cold that sets in once dusk falls; by noon tomorrow they will have made it no further than the next fleck of sun. It is silent except for the rush of water and a few resident birds chirping and quarrelling, searching for sustenance. Over the embankment leading down to the stony riverbed hang the brown umbels of butterfly bushes past bloom. A small roadway-landscaper's van pulls up. Three men get out, adjust their orange protective clothing, survey the land. With a few hand movements they unmount the trail signs erected for venturesome day trippers: to the bitumen mine, to the mountain huts and climbable peaks, as well as one or two information boards about the local nature sanctuary. It is now a time for hibernation somewhere protected from the endless rain, snow, and frost. They will move the signs into storage, perhaps in the small mine museum, where the tired faces of famished mountain people from the last two centuries look out at the rare visitor in warm sepia tones, much like in the knife grinders' museum where the black-clad, thin and bitter women hunched beneath panniers pose beside the playful knife grinder men before they set out into the open. In winter, these crooked gazes – bathed in warm museum light – are also disguised behind the trail signs stored there to keep from weathering.

Now the men remove large pieces of equipment from the back of the van and begin to stride back and forth, as if armed, past the strips of green sparsely planted with trees, before pausing. They start up their leaf blowers, revving the engines several times, and then, holding them very close to the ground, move them back and forth, as if to prove to one another that they know what they're doing. Then they turn them off. Two of the men put their equipment back in the van, briefly discuss something with the third man, who remains standing in the road, and then climb back in and drive off. The remaining man stands there awhile, trying to start his blower's engine, which repeatedly stutters, but eventually drones uniformly. The landscaped area at the river is sparsely covered with recently planted trees. The young trees' thin foliage is already yellow after a dry summer and the air movement from the machine causes single leaves to fall to the ground. With his droning blower, the man endeavours to shoo the few fallen leaves into a pile on the landscaped area. The yellow and brownish leaves on the grass, wet from dew, do not want to cooperate; they want to be a flock or an imagined herd, they whirl in here and out there, dance out of the row and want to be left in peace. The motor saws into the quiet morning over the riverbed, and the council worker might ask himself, why? Why a groomed, park-like state of order that lasts into the winter should be achieved, only here, on this spot of grass, while the chalk cliffs, always ready to trickle, the trees and bushes on the bank and hillsides, the dark winter rose leaves in the shadowy bends and embankments, the small bluish cyclamen shoots, and above all the water, in its clear and turquoise courses and sways, whose currents rush so differently in summer, while they should all be allowed to follow their own rules, tarnished not by a single interference. The ornery leaves spread further and further and more sparsely over the surface of the lawn. The man turns off his machine and puts it away in a kind of protective shaft. He stands at the edge of the small row of trees, smoking, his gaze welded to the surface of the lawn, until the van returns and he's allowed to climb in with the others. For a while the vehicle idles in the road, and all three sit in the front seat, leaning forward, gazing at the thin trees, the manicured strips of grass, the splayed foliage – a sight worth keeping in mind, in case they are required to account for their performance of this morning.

They leave the valley heading for the *statale*, and should one of them happen to look in the rearview mirror, he might, like some travellers before him, be under the impression that the valley closes behind him.

OLGA

One day the little cat was dead. She lay utterly still in the yard. Behind her ear was a wound, as if from a stone; her little skull was broken. To this day I think it was the neighbour's children. They were always up to mischief. They were always catching animals – snakes, mice, birds, insects – and getting up to no good with them, and stones often flew when they were around. Their aim was precise, they could even hit a bird in flight. During the second

204

earthquake I wished a stone would fall on their heads.

It came in September, the second earthquake. Or to be precise: several earthquakes. It lasted a few days, but at first it was only a trembling accompanied by a very distant lumber. It began in the morning. Everyone already stood outside, in front of their houses, some still in their nightgowns, and all of a sudden it became so silent, so silent, as it never is in the world, as if everyone in the village held their breath, and even the birds kept silent. A few things fell over – in the shed, in the house, small things – and then came two or three days of peace. But then, in the bright light of midday, it began to rumble again as it had back in May, after a cold burst of wind and with this yellow fog in the sky. It finished off other villages in the valley. Bell towers that were only half-standing collapsed entirely, and the rest of the houses did as well. In our house everything that we had rebuilt remained standing, and the church tower held this time, too. It was shortly before noon. Our bell tower was the only one in the entire valley that rang. But old things that had survived the first earthquake now caved in. Sheds, houses, nearly all the remaining huts up in the mountain pastures. The cracks might have been there already, hidden and invisible. Just waiting for the next earthquake. Many people were very afraid. I wasn't afraid, but I knew I didn't want to stay any longer in the valley.

LINA

My younger sister fell in love with a soldier. It couldn't not have happened, I thought. They arrived like heroes and saviours, and everyone worshipped them. Only a few men groused – that it took too long, that they were worthless, lazy, and so on. But everyone else was happy they came and they were quick, too: with the field kitchen, distributing mattresses and blankets and sleeping bags, pitching tents, they did all that well. They had to. And my sister fell for one of them, they were always flirting, she was still so young. She was training to become a seamstress when the earthquake hit; it was a good profession, back then there was even work around us. Seamstresses are always in demand, my mother said, and moreover, she could learn the trade in the chief village and didn't have to leave. At the sewing competition before a live audience – *The Making of a Shirt*, it was called – she even won first prize: she was the quickest, and highly accurate. At any rate, their infatuation took its course, and one morning the fellow was withdrawn along with his unit. She cried and was heartbroken and waited for a letter, it was hard to watch. Then she became very quiet. She always crept behind me, helping out wherever she could – something new. And then, while we sorted beans, she told me. She was pregnant. And she didn't even know his last name. I immediately gave her all the advice I could. Red wine with parsley, a sitz bath in soapy water, try jumping from the table, but nothing worked. And then came the earthquake. In September. A few shocks – everyone was in a flurry of excitement, but it was nothing. We comforted ourselves thinking, maybe it was just a little after-burp of May, and now it's quiet. But then it came back. It was noon. A bright day. Overcast, but it's often hazy around here in Indian summer. And then again came such a sharp, icy gust of wind, as in May, and this rumbling. This rumbling from that animal below our feet that moves and turns itself around so, making the Earth sway and roof tiles fall, and what was almost fully constructed fell back down. We had luck with our house this time, too. And my sister had luck, because in all the back and forth and

206

horror and fear, she lost what was in her belly. She told me the next evening, she had bled badly, but was already feeling better, and she laughed and cried, it was all such a horror.

ANSELMO

My grandmother went to the cemetery increasingly often. I don't know what she did there. She would drop whatever she was doing, around the house or out in the field, and head off. Food burned, the fire died, tomatoes went rotten because she left them outside in a basket in the rain. When early one morning such a trembling ran through the ground again and everything clattered, she, too, went off. A neighbour found her in the morning and took her home: she had been sitting at the bus station. Yet she never rode the bus. Then she was nervous for a few days, always talking to herself, but she stayed indoors and cooked, harvested the beans. And then all of a sudden she was gone again. My father became angry, but never went looking for her. On that day we had to sort the beans. Shell them, separate them. Good, bad. Big, small. Neither of us took care, my sister and I. We kicked each other's shins below the table. It was fun and we laughed, until it started to hurt. Suddenly my father came in from outside and saw the beans lying jumbled in a heap. He hollered and smacked us, then we had to kneel in a corner, facing the wall. That was something new he'd thought up. We had to kneel there in the corner and later, at his command, scoot over to him on our knees and beg forgiveness. I never did it, but my sister did – she was always hungry, and if we didn't do it there would be nothing to eat, he said. Sometimes he forgot about it. On that day we had been kneeling in the corner for maybe half an hour when the roaring began. Just as in May. Outside a sudden wind blew, causing the window to slam shut, breaking the pane, or maybe it was already broken from the first shock. We both jumped up and walked outside. Everything happened at the same time, somehow, as it had in May. But how the Earth trembled below my knees – I still remember it. My grandmother stood in the yard and screamed.

SILVIA

I had only been home for a few days when the new earthquake began. A tottering, of sorts, without thunder, but everyone went outside right away, early in the morning. I remember it better than the second one. After school I got a job in Milan, and I had a room behind the train station, in a house directly on the metro line. My room was on the third floor, and whenever the train drove past below the house I could feel the trembling, and I always thought back to that first earthquake in September. In Milan sometimes I asked myself what it would be like, to live through an earthquake in a house like that – five, six stories high with floors so thin and the ceilings too, on every floor I could hear children crying, I was exactly in the middle.

TONI

I was happy that lessons were about to start again. The school itself wasn't rebuilt yet; it was in the chief village, which had been completely destroyed. But here in our village a building was finished, where everyone was supposed to go. There were few of us in the valley. But the second earthquake put an end to all that. It was different than in May. There had been a warning a few days prior. But no one wanted to believe it would be that bad again. It was as if everyone thought: Oh, the monster was only dreaming or tossing lightly in its sleep.

MARA

Before the wedding it happened again. In September. A small one; it was morning, I think, and it scared us well enough, yet caused no further damage. But then a few days later the behemoth roared again, at around noon, while I stood in the yard and all of a sudden the sky turned yellow, and it was as if all sound had been sponged up – a silence, what a silence, followed by this roaring, as it had roared already in May. Luna jumped around like a small animal, her eyes open wide in horror; where was my brother, where was my brother? Then she clung to me. My brother sat in the shed repairing umbrellas – his trade alongside knife grinding – maybe he planned to hit the road again on his bicycle. He had a tough time getting out of the shed. I thought about my mother, how she lay there in the grave while the ground beneath us rumbled.

SILVIA

The second big quake came that afternoon. Around us school wasn't back in session yet. I don't remember what I was doing at that moment, but I think I was outside in the yard. My grandmother grabbed hold of me and then we stood in the road. My father wasn't with us. Thank God it's daytime, I thought, I still remember that today. And I wondered whether my father would still go to the factory. It was supposed to open again. For the last few days he had been grinding knives in the valley, and people were bringing him umbrellas to repair before autumn, he'd had enough.

GIGI

This rumbling inflicted a wound on all who lived through the earthquake. A scar has remained that will never go away. For some of us it is small and hidden, while for others it is out in the open, like a white raised lip from a hand slipped while hacking wood. Afterwards, after this wound, we all had to start over from the beginning: we were like children, aside from the fact that we adults already had a life behind us that we still remembered. But we had to start over with almost everything. Work, the neighbourhood, the animals, music – all that was now divided into the before and after.

But then it happened again. It was in September. It began mildly, at dawn, and the goats stood stock-still; I checked on them right away. Then came a powerful one. The days between were hushed. We thought it was already over after the first mild quake. We were lucky, we thought. Yet in a way we were waiting for it. Two or three days passed. Then, at noon, such a deep rumbling came again. But it came from a different direction than it had in May – I'm very sure of that. As if it'd rolled in from Monte Musi. The sky was overcast, but it was warm. I had just made plans with my neighbour to fell timber the next day.

ANSELMO

The second earthquake came without a portent. The dogs did not bark or howl, and there was nothing unusual about the weather, at least not that I noticed. I can no longer say which earthquake was worse. The first or the

210

second. You can't compare them. What's worse: an earthquake comes when you've never given one any thought, or an earthquake comes when you still know exactly what it means, and have just finished putting everything back in order? Not everything, of course – a lot of things were still broken – but no one around us was living in tents any more. Yes, how to say what is worse?

TONI

At the end of summer the backhoes and bulldozers returned, mostly to the chief village. This time I already knew the men and was happy to help. I didn't know what to do at home. And it was fun working with them, they practically treated me like an adult. A few times they even gave me cigarettes. One day they said, We're clearing out the rubble. Out, meaning out of the valley. I didn't know where they would take it. I begged the one driver to let me come along. He consented, there were three of us in the cab. The driver was in a big hurry. He drove very quickly, the trailer lurching from side to side in the curves downhill. And then below, on the flat road, maybe around halfway to the valley exit he skidded off the road. Luckily we landed in the bushes, there was no drop. But the entire truck hung crookedly in the brush, and the rubble had already fallen halfway out of the trailer into the scrub. I don't know why it happened, whether it was already because of the earthquake, at all events we hung crookedly in the cab, and below us the Earth quaked and I saw a stone avalanche descend the north face of Monte Plauris. I don't know if that was the sound I heard, or if it was thunder, but in any case I was afraid. We had to climb out the driver's door on top, and I ran off, up the road, taking the shortcut through the forest; I just ran and I was

211

afraid that an abyss would suddenly open up or I would find our village lying utterly in ruins.

OLGA

After the second earthquake, they said: We can evacuate you. Again the soldiers, fire department, civil defence. Whoever had relatives willing to take them in should leave, regardless of where they lived. Many ended up far away, all the way in Turin, Genoa, Bologna. Above all the children should go. They had to go to school. Many mothers went along with their children, and grandmothers. They could go to the seaside, to vacation rentals. Lignano, Bibione, Grado. The holidays were over. The government organized it all. There was a lot of moaning and wailing – the elderly didn't want to go – but I also signed myself up for the bus. My father stood at my side in line. I couldn't tell if he was sad, but then, when it was my turn, he said to me: Come back, my daughter, be well and don't forget me. That made me cry, and I cried the entire ride through the valley, as we passed by the devastated towns, trails left by rock slides, the craggy hillsides, the river. That entire earthquake summer, I hadn't left. From the bus I saw Venzone again. Gemona. The rubble.

LINA

My youngest sister was only twelve. A very late addition. We gave her to relatives, a cousin of my mother, down in the plains. I think whoever took in an earthquake child received money. At any rate she was quick to say yes, and Maria-Rosa got on the bus, and our relatives picked her up in Udine, or somewhere even closer to the sea. Many children went away back then. They stayed away for at

212

least a year. We missed her, our baby, but it was better for us. None of the children who went to school down there wanted to stay in the valley afterwards. After finishing school my little sister went away, too. She wanted to become a hairdresser. Our mother had died, things had got easier. The streets were all smoothly paved and the damages from the earthquake had been repaired, and they built us a museum, and in general everything was on the up. She found work at the cardboard box factory.

SILVIA

Shortly after the earthquake my mother arrived. She brought with her the mouldy suitcase. It had already been decided who would go to the seaside and who would go elsewhere. If your house had earthquake damages you could move into an apartment or hotel at the seaside. The holidays were over. My grandmother also came along, my father stayed behind. Since everything had to be rebuilt. We were given an apartment in a high tower, you could even see a bit of the ocean, we were on the seventh floor. Other children from our valley went to our school there, and lived in our building as well. At first all we did was ride the elevator, but later we also played at the beach, the lounge chairs and umbrellas had all been cleared away. And we played in the small park with the fountain, shut off in winter. Everything was different in winter. The bumper car arena was closed and so were all the toy shops, and even the ice cream parlours. There wasn't any music playing anywhere. My mother continued to work in the hotel for a bit. Off-season, she said. Now the cheapskates come. She meant the Austrians. And the Germans. Childless. My mother showed my grandmother where to stand and look in order to see the mountains. On the other side of the corridor by the elevator was a window from floor to ceiling. When the weather was nice you saw past the park trees and the roofs of the houses, all the way to the mountains. But my grandmother didn't want to stand by the window. It always made her so dizzy. At Christmas my father visited.

ANSELMO

The renovated school room was useless. School couldn't begin, and some had lost the roof over their heads. Now the message was, get out of the valley if you can. I was sent to an uncle in Gonars. Down in the plains. Almost at the sea, but from there you couldn't see the water yet. Everything was flat. Where my sister went, I can't remember. Be careful they don't send you to that camp, a neighbour said, when he heard where I was going. He meant the concentration camp for Slavs. But nothing like that existed any more.

TONI

After a few days, once the streets had been cleared, my mother took my sister and me away from the valley. We were bussed to the seaside. You're getting your trip to the seaside after all, my father said to my mother, as a joke, but she cried. Many people cried, I think. The holidays were over and we could live in vacation rentals. In the high rise where we stayed, there were also other families from our village. At first we thought it was great, the elevator and all those stairs, and the sea. But later there was a lot of bickering among the adults. I also made a new friend, from Venzone. He had been buried beneath the rubble. Together with his grandmother, and that's how she died.

214

But he told me that only once. I never asked him about it, although I wanted to know more. But he was a good pal, and there at the sea he was my best friend. We talked a lot. About girls and things. And what we wanted to do. I told him about Moscow, he knew nothing about Russia.

MARA

Tiles fell from the roofs again, barns broke to pieces, walls collapsed. Who could grasp a thing like this. After that people simply wanted to leave. As soon as the roads were clear buses came to pick people up and take them to faraway places. And many never returned. They searched for a new life, built one. My brother left, too, with his bride. They stood in line for the bus, by the cemetery. The families with children had priority, since the children had to be in school. She was very small beside my brother, Luna. Like a child seen from behind, with her small crooked suitcase. They waved to me from the bus as it drove off. Then they went abroad; occasionally they send me a postcard, and once my brother even sent money, for the gravestone.

OLGA

I never wanted to go back. I wanted my father to come live with me; he visited, but didn't want to stay. I have a good job, in Mestre, in a factory. Been there for years. I'm in the office, not on the assembly line. I have a small apartment with a balcony. In the evenings and mornings I hear the airplanes. My neighbour always complains, but it doesn't bother me one bit. In the factory you can't hear it at all. Then my aunt passed away. My father is old. After spending years away, I returned to the valley. Everything had changed, even the mountains. Yes, and I liked all the questions. The fact that people would occasionally ask me: What was it like here in the valley back then, during the earthquake? What was it like here in the valley, in general? No one asked me that anywhere else – but you have to get it off your chest, this memory. Even if few people want to talk about it now, they all still have them, their memories. Of this rumbling. And everything altogether.

ANSELMO

It was a nice year, there in Gonars. The land is so flat. The big fields. Not a single hill. The long paths, lanes. My uncle was nice, as was his wife. I think they got money to take me in, but they never let me feel it. I was given a bicycle. My uncle was an electrician; sometimes he took me along and I had to help out, but only a little. Handing him tools, collecting trash after a job, sweeping up. It didn't interest me, but I was happy to do it anyway. Once my mother came to visit. It was a surprise. But my uncle knew about it ahead of time. She came with her new boyfriend, by car, and she rented a room. We drove to Grado and spent time at the seaside, it was off season, we could sit on the beach where it smelled strongly of algae from the last storm. I fed the seagulls cookies; after that they didn't leave me alone. My mother's boyfriend was Calabrian, he taught me a few card tricks, and to this day I can remember how short his fingers were, shorter than mine, but he was so quick and nimble, he knew every trick. It was a nice visit. After she left, my uncle said: Don't tell your father. I didn't see my father that entire school year. I was not happy to go back. I hadn't missed anything while I was out there in the plains. Not a thing.

TONI

Shortly before Christmas my father came and picked us up. He had found an apartment on the outskirts of Udine, and already before Christmas we moved in. He hadn't said a word about it ahead of time, not even to my mother. That was worse than the earthquake. He had brought a few things with him from our house, which stood in boxes in the hallway. Everything else was either a donation or something he'd just bought. He had got money from somewhere, from the government or from his labour union; he had a good job at a factory in Udine. Other families from the valley lived in the tower apartments as well. They were always sitting around together – at our place, too – discussing life up there in the valley. In the towers people always referred to us as 'the Russians'. Most of them took us for idiots, I think. Held back. At least that's how they treated us. During summer vacations we worked on our house, and after two years we moved back in. Some people never moved back. They stayed in the apartments and only came to the valley in summer, for celebrations, or for carnival. And then there were always accidents afterwards, since they were no longer accustomed to the tight, steep curves. In the course of this a few of them checked out.

MARA

After the earthquake the cemetery was in complete disarray again. All the work had been in vain. The crosses stood every which way, gravestones had toppled. I would have liked to go with my brother to get the photo plaque made for my mother's gravestone, but we never got around to it.

From our entire family now the only thing left here in

the house is my brother's knife grinder's bicycle, and his bag with knives for sale and the tools he used for grinding. And me.

GIGI

Things that had just been restored collapsed. And houses that people had considered rescued now developed large cracks. Everyone had spent the entire summer working on their houses, and now so much was lost again. Many people left then, especially those with children. Whoever had relatives outside, in the plains, in a different part of the country, sent their children there. There were also people out there who took in children they weren't related to. Many people wanted to go abroad. Just get away. The valley was emptied out again. And only a few returned. That's how it was in the earthquake year. The entire valley was jolted and shaken, and nothing returned to how it had been before. In the end you couldn't even say whether the stones and boulders in the river had been there always, or only since the earthquake.

What is an earthquake? An earthquake – it's as if something enormous were moving in a dream. Or as if a giant were uneasy in its sleep. And waking up, it creates a new order of things in the world. Then the human being with their life becomes small as the smallest pebble in the river.

LINA

Below, from my stand, I watch the world go on. Destroyed Venzone has been rebuilt so beautifully. With so much love and effort, and you don't even see any more that it was once a pile of rubble. Only a few things were left in such a state, as if in memorial. A few archways without a building, remnants of walls. Yet it's not wild and over-grown, but immaculate. Now the street is so wide. And all the new developments alongside the road. Comfortable houses with large terraces, certainly a nice bathroom in each one. The old rubble has almost grown together.

Between the road and the river are meadows and a field, I walk around there occasionally when I have a lot of time before the bus comes. Once there was a flock of white birds, of a kind I'd never seen before. They flew in like a cloud and all settled down on the field, they were large and very thin, with long necks. They flew past like birds from a fairy tale or a foreign land. They walked around entirely without fear, without looking around, as if they didn't have to watch out for any danger, but when I got a bit nearer they flew off at once, drifting closer to the river. A man biked over and I stopped him to ask about the birds, they're called egrets. I don't think our language has a word for egret.

OLGA

Sometimes I wake up in the night feeling as if my mouth were full of dust. The taste of mortar dust and chalk. Now I will suffocate, I think, now I am buried below the rubble and will suffocate. In my nose and in my mouth I still have this memory, as if it were embossed, and I can never be sure when it will awaken. However that may be, something wakes it, sometimes while I'm sleeping, some-times abruptly in the middle of the day, at work, while I'm watching television. But it always passes, and I don't suffocate.

VII

'Happy, then, are the mountain people, whom fate has dealt a seemingly unfavourable dwelling place between the Alps. They will become the new seedbed of the human race; conquerors without bloodshed, they will come to possess the plains ravaged by the floods.'
— Peter Simon Pallas, *On the Structure of the Mountains and the Transformations of the Globe* (1777)

SADDLE

Should the valley ever actually close at its exit to Statale 13, there is a way out. It is arduous and rugged and leads from the entrance to the former bitumen mine, across a repeatedly obliterated, buried, partway-blocked footpath, onto an alpine pasture. One has to use their hands and feet on this trail, its accessibility doubtful, the gaze always averted from the abyss, ears closed to the steady gnarling of scree. Like a phantasm of mellifluousness, the pasture lies waiting at the end of this first stretch, surrounded by harsh cliffs, as if they were appointed guardians of the horizon, their faces revealing the buckling and the tremors, the injuries that lent them their form. One has to wonder how livestock could have ever possibly found their way up here, in order to graze on this green, aside from perhaps goats, nimble-footed in the mountains. It leads out of the pasture onto a pass, from where a yonder appears tangible in bright, clear light; a strip of lustre like the horizon to the south, and against this backdrop, it appears as if one could fly across the low rocky hills and the green distant Venzonassa valley. That's how easy it is to forget the many obstacles that cannot be weighed, presented by the various towering rocks. But it is still a far way to go, a beautiful exercise in balance between harshness and distance on the southside of Monte Plauris, until at last the bright delta also comes into view, the confluence of the Fella and Tagliamento, the dazzling field of stones, the thin shimmering veins of water in white and turquoise, already indicating that the opening grows near, the erosion of the mountains, the stone deterioration all the way to the sea. Hill country.

Downhill into the Venzonassa valley. Green, silent, here in summer the oriole calls in the open woodlands interrupted by small rocky shims of limestone. The church tower of Venzone indicates the direction that must remain untraversed on one's right, and the Tagliamento and the dark wall of Monte San Simeone on the shore beyond. The valley is streaked by islands of heather where in summer the heat broods, soil of sand, clay, and shards; it is edged by bleak, roundly fissured single mountains, sparsely forested and presenting themselves higher than they actually are; it is said that the earthquakes altered the shape of their peaks. Over the yellowish scree bed of a lost river or brook, it leads back uphill, past the Creta Storta – crooked ridge or crooked chalk, a stone yellow-reddish with a disharmonic fold, roundly layered in wavy lines, brightly grained, finished with spiky edges on the east, sparsely forested all the way to the upper edge on the south, as if covered in a shaggy, dark fur. A picture book of the shifts and interferences, a testimony to the *dislocations* of the various layers of rock. The wall accompanies the path on the eastern side, to Sella di Sant'Agnese, the final opening, the saddle and the exit over the mountain, where all at once the open land lies spread out at the beholder's feet, the shadows of purple-grey slopes still on the left – when seen from the south they oppose the gaze, so forbidding and sombre. The plain almost always lies in mist, as mist often lies above moraine landscapes, a blurred field of light broken here and there by low, dark outgrowths – final displaced attempts at forming mountains, which lie there like sleeping animals in the brightness, yet achieve nothing more against the horizon. And there, on the horizon: a visible strip shimmering between violet, a reddish tone, orange and a thin stroke of blinding silver – the sea.

SKY

Between the Tagliamento and Isonzo rivers, the Adriatic coastline connects to a broad plain, whose soil is punctuated by stones and pebbles that grow ever smaller towards the south, and which naturally ends in the broad, flat sand beach that, edged here and there by pine forests, ushers in the calm sea. On the sandy, pebbly ground of the plain that is petering out, they have built coastal resorts; it is an increasingly sprawling seasonal terrain where noisy summers are balanced out by the languid calm of the rainy autumn and winter months – that is, if there is such a thing as equilibrium on the scale of roaring sound and silence.

Autumn and winter are times of vacancy at the sea, times of shops shuttered and locked, of dark hotel windows, of closed curtains, of the last small testaments to pleasantries in the form of colourful snips of entrance tickets, chocolate wrappers, thrown-away postcards flitting over the unswept lanes at the will of the wind. Even the street sweepers have been told to stay home, and the seasonal workers are dormant or doing their winter jobs in more or less distant hometowns.

That autumn and winter after the earthquake, things were different. The draughty apartments and hotel rooms, anything but cosy in winter, were occupied. Countless partial and half-families from the earthquake region in the Alpine foothills – a landscape that on clear days was visible from the north-facing windows of the hotel apartments, in misty blue tones with white peak-marks drawn against the sky – were put up here, so they would have a roof over their heads to keep out the rain, cold, snow. In towns where otherwise few children lived, the children went to the schools, hastily equipped for additional students. The mothers might have looked for work

224

here and there. They certainly needed more saleswomen, cooks, cleaning women, even office employees, than they had in other winters. The grandmothers cooked, pressed themselves against the cold glass panes in order to catch a glimpse of the sea, or the mountains when the sun was shining. The fathers stayed at home and confronted the rubble, while the grandfathers, as a rule, had already been resting in the grave for a long time. The seagulls soon turned up again, which in winter usually resorted to more fertile strips of coast; they soared past the windows of the hotel apartments and filled the air with their cries. The children played in the parks withered by autumn, and, on the beach, where they threw wet algae at one another, tossed balls back and forth, played cards between the rows of changing booths, where they were protected from the wind. In the cover of locked beach toilets, groups of adolescent girls whispered secrets – about boys – and below the roof of an unused bus stop, the boys laughed, embarrassed – about girls. Arching above them all was the massive – and most of the time, grey – sky of the Adriatic foreland basin, as geologists refer to this broad plain traversed by rows of willows and mulberries, wild rose hedges, hawthorn and elderflower, sunken rubble of former mountains, supplanted, displaced masses, carried from higher positions by glacial melting. In the afternoon the grandmothers met on the beach promenade, always dressed in black, wearing headscarves, and in the black slippers traditional to the valley, scuffled across the smooth pavement slabs. They stood at the point where, between the changing booths and the fences, there was a view to the ocean, and occasionally they brought a hand to their forehead, bending their arm at a right angle, as if to shield themselves from the sun. There was the sea: grey, at times blue, at times green, opaque, rarely rough, the legendary home of Riba Faronika, who in the end, it could not be denied, was responsible for all this. But they said nothing about it, not even to one another, and they didn't sing either, not even quietly, because it was too late for that – and even had they hummed, out of homesickness or simply from memory, never would they have moved their hands up and down before their breast, imitating a wave or a snake: not here, beneath this endless sky and in the presence of the horizon.

MEMORIAL

In the course of both earthquakes, of May and of September 1976, the cathedral in Venzone was largely destroyed. For the reconstruction they numbered the salvaged stones and laid them out on the massive gravel field that had formed at the confluence of two rivers: the Tagliamento, coming from the west, and the Fella, from the north. The Fella brings along the white stones, from the chalky mountains north-east of Venzone; the Tagliamento brings chunks of sediment and metamorphic rock from the Dolomite foothills. The gravel field at the confluence is hardly ever submerged in water, only rivulets run through it, swelling after heavy rains. Although the Tagliamento is larger and contributes more diverse stones, the white of the chalk dominates the gravel field and is blinding in the sun.

As they laid out and ordered the stones, they found markings on the individual blocks and hewn pieces of rock – indicating what building part, cardinal direction, type of stone and size – left behind centuries ago by the stonemasons and their workshops. Invisible in a state of completion, as they disappeared inside the joints, and certainly not made in mind with the prospect of the

226

building breaking to pieces, and yet there they are: an inscription, safeguarded and safeguarding from erasure, secret testimonies of authorship.

Stone by stone and piece by piece, the cathedral in Venzone was reconstructed. Cracks, displacements, damages remained visible, holes were left unconcealed. Every such trace should serve in memory of the destruction that came before the reconstruction.

Now in the chancel of the church there is a long, rescued strip of a destroyed fresco, covered in symbols like those pilgrims left behind for centuries, in agreed-upon locations in the sites they visited. On stone benches, in parts of church walls, on the backs of icons, on the lower edges of fresco panels, the objects of worship, the goal or step in the pilgrim or seeker's journey. The image that was regarded as either the end point of the pilgrimage itself or a step along the way, has been lost; the marginalia has remained. Left is a reel of pilgrims' testimonials; foreign and nameless, they wanted to write themselves in although they could not write – they remain in the memory of this place, they who wanted to brace themselves against oblivion with a sign. A rite that, in its plea for memory and commemoration, perhaps no pilgrim was aware of, but which nevertheless remained a followed custom, an expression of a silent, unarticulated – if anything, unconscious – desire to be seen. Heard in the sign. A manifold 'Here I am,' in answer to the biblical call for the present, for presence. And a call itself, an invocation of the memory of this place. An indecipherable reel of signs, a crumbling narrative of implied images encrypted by time, concerned with the task of remembrance.

NOTES

The illustrations show sections of the surviving fresco in the cathedral at Venzone.

The epigraph on page 5 in translation:

> And then the dark plain shook so violently
> that I start to bathe in sweat all over again
> reliving the terror in my memory.
> Up from the tear-soaked ground a great wind ran,
> flashing a bright red light out of its swell
> that blasted all my senses…

Dante Alighieri, *Inferno*. Translated by Michael Palma. New York: W. W. Norton & Company, 2008.

Page 7
Friedrich Hoffmann, *Geschichte der Geognosie und Schilderung der Vulkanischen Erscheinungen*, p. 328

Page 57
Carl Friedrich Naumann, *Lehrbuch der Geognosie*, vol. 1, pp. 206–208

Page 93
Eduard Suess, *The Face of the Earth*, vol. 1, translated by Herta BC Sollas and William Johnson Sollas, Oxford: Clarendon Press, 1904, p. 179

Page 125
Eduard Suess, *The Face of the Earth*, vol. 1, translated by Herta BC Sollas and William Johnson Sollas, Oxford: Clarendon Press, 1904, p. 270, 278

Page 165
Carl Friedrich Naumann, *Lehrbuch der Geognosie*, vol. 1, p. 673

Page 201
Eduard Suess, *The Face of the Earth*, vol. 1, translated by Herta BC Sollas and William Johnson Sollas, Oxford: Clarendon Press, 1904, p. 74

Page 221
Peter Simon Pallas, *Über die Beschaffenheit der Gebirge und die Veränderungen der Erdkugel*, p. 87

The fairy tales 'Fable' (p. 43) and 'Tale of the Shirt' (p. 104) are very loose adaptions of stories from *Fiabe italiane* by Italo Calvino.

ESTHER KINSKY grew up by the Rhine River and lived in London for twelve years. She is the author of six volumes of poetry; five novels (*Summer Resort, Banatsko, River, Grove, Rombo*); numerous essays on language, poetry, and translation; and three children's books. She has translated many notable English (John Clare, Henry David Thoreau, Iain Sinclair) and Polish (Joanna Bator, Miron Białoszewski, Magdalena Tulli) authors into German. Both *River* and *Grove* won numerous literary prizes in Germany. *Rombo* was awarded the newly founded W.-G.-Sebald-Literaturpreis in 2020. In 2022, Kinsky was awarded the prestigious Kleist Prize for her oeuvre.

CAROLINE SCHMIDT was born in Princeton, New Jersey. She translated Esther Kinsky's *Grove* and has translated poetry by Friederike Mayröcker, and art historical essays, museum catalogues, and exhibition texts for Albertina in Vienna and Pinakothek der Moderne in Munich, among others. She lives in Berlin.